ALSO BY M A COMLEY

Blind Justice (Novella)

Cruel Justice (Book #1)

Mortal Justice (Novella)

Impeding Justice (Book #2)

Final Justice (Book #3)

Foul Justice (Book #4)

Guaranteed Justice (Book #5)

Ultimate Justice (Book #6)

Virtual Justice (Book #7)

Hostile Justice (Book #8)

Tortured Justice (Book #9)

Rough Justice (Book #10)

Dubious Justice (Book #11)

Calculated Justice (Book #12)

Twisted Justice (Book #13)

Justice at Christmas (Short Story)

Justice at Christmas 2 (novella)

Prime Justice (Book #14)

Heroic Justice (Book #15)

Shameful Justice (Book #16)

Immoral Justice (Book #17)

Toxic Justice (Book #18)

Overdue Justice (Book #19)

Unfair Justice (a 10,000 word short story)

Torn Apart (Hero series #1)

End Result (Hero series #2)

In Plain Sight (Hero Series #3)

Double Jeopardy (Hero Series #4)

Criminal Actions (Hero Series #5) Coming January 2020

Sole Intention (Intention series #1)

Grave Intention (Intention series #2)

Devious Intention (Intention #3)

Merry Widow (A Lorne Simpkins short story)

It's A Dog's Life (A Lorne Simpkins short story)

A Time To Heal (A Sweet Romance)

A Time For Change (A Sweet Romance)

High Spirits

The Temptation series (Romantic Suspense/New Adult Novellas)

Past Temptation

Lost Temptation

Cozy Mystery Series

Murder at the Wedding

Murder at the Hotel

Murder by the Sea

Tempting Christa (A billionaire romantic suspense co-authored by Tracie Delaney #1)

Avenging Christa (A billionaire romantic suspense co-authored by Tracie Delaney #2)

ACKNOWLEDGMENTS

Thank you as always to my rock, Jean, I'd be lost without you in my life.

Special thanks as always go to @studioenp for their superb cover design expertise.

My heartfelt thanks go to my wonderful editor Emmy Ellis, my proofreaders Joseph, Barbara and Jacqueline for spotting all the lingering nits.

Mary, you're always in my thoughts. Miss you dearly.

KEEP IN TOUCH WITH THE AUTHOR

Twitter
https://twitter.com/Melcom1

Blog
http://melcomley.blogspot.com

Facebook
http://smarturl.it/sps7jh

Newsletter
http://smarturl.it/8jtcvv

BookBub
www.bookbub.com/authors/m-a-comley

MURDER BY THE SEA

Carmel Cove Cozy Mysteries Book 3

1

*T*he wind whipped around her face. Ruth was used to the sea breeze, but this was something different. She was concerned about their safety and called her four-legged companion, Ben, to heel.

"We'd better go back, boy. This weather would freeze the whatnots off a brass monkey."

Ben peered up at her and barked his agreement.

That was the trouble living by the sea. While it was beautiful in the summer to stroll along the coastal path, it was a darn sight riskier in the winter months. She had reached the exact same point where her dear friend, Geraldine, had slipped over the edge a few months earlier and had to be rescued by the coastguard and local rescue team. This validated her decision to call it a day.

It was no great hardship. Ben loved it at the village green anyway. He generally spent most of his playtime down there either chasing the squirrels from tree to tree or sniffing around the other dogs.

It wasn't until they got back to the car that Ruth realised she had missed a call on her mobile. "Damn wind, I couldn't hear myself think up there, boy. I won't delay your romp at the park for long, I promise."

The call was from her mother who had supposedly set off on one of her many adventures with Ruth's father in their campervan. She hit the

Return Call button and waited. "Mum, sorry for not getting back to you right away, we were up on the coastal path and I didn't hear the phone ring. Is everything all right?"

"First of all, why the dickens were you up there in this atrocious weather? I would have thought a woman with your intelligence would know to steer clear of a treacherous place like that during a storm."

Me and my big mouth. "It's not stormy, Mum. It's blustery at best, but definitely not stormy, otherwise I wouldn't be up here. Anyway, that's beside the point. What's wrong? What have you forgotten?"

Her mother let out a long-suffering sigh. "Everything has gone wrong. Your father is out there now trying to fix the damn thing."

"Fix what? You're not making any sense."

Her mother, Wilma, was a retired GP, and since her retirement she'd been prone to blowing things up out of all proportion. Ruth wondered if it was to fill a void in her life, perhaps even out of necessity to belong to the community. She was aware how harsh that sounded, but it was the truth. Her father had turned out to be the steadying force in the relationship, since he'd given up work as a renowned heart surgeon a few years earlier.

"The campervan. It's broken down on the way to Scotland."

"Oh no, where? You couldn't have got very far."

"Precisely thirty-three miles. I urged your father to get it serviced, but as usual, anything to do with the vehicles he deemed beyond my realms of capabilities or intelligence. Well, I was right. We're stuck on a country lane now because he insisted on taking the scenic route."

"Mum, there's no point apportioning blame, that's not going to help the situation. I take it Dad has rung the breakdown service?"

"He has, and guess what?"

Ruth closed her eyes, fearing what her mother was about to say next. She had an inkling it was going to be bad news, judging by the tone of her voice. "Surprise me?"

"It ran out last month, and your father never got around to renewing the policy."

"You're kidding me. Crikey, just because you're both retired now that doesn't mean you can give your brain cells a rest."

"Don't you think I told your father that? I rang you for help, dear, not a lecture. Are you prepared to help us or do I need to call someone else?" An exasperated *tut* and an expelled frustrated breath trickled into her ear.

"I'm sorry. I didn't mean to do that, Mum. Heck, what can I do? It's not as if I'm a fully trained mechanic or anything like that."

"You can come and rescue me for a start. I refuse to spend a moment longer here with your father."

"Don't tell me you two have fallen out over this?"

"Okay, I won't tell you that, except I'd be lying. Are you going to come out and get me or do I have to ring your sister and lay all this at her door?"

"No, don't bother Carolyn, you know she and Keith are trying to finish off all the snagging at the cottage. I'll come. You're going to have to give me a postcode for your location. I'm useless without my satnav for guidance."

"Don't go asking me that. I'm hopeless at that type of thing."

"Then you're going to have to ask Dad, aren't you?"

"I would if I was speaking to him."

"Mother! Either you want my help or you don't. Get off your high horse and find out the information I need to come and fetch you."

Her mother grumbled something incoherent, and Ruth heard her unclip her seat belt and get out of the car. The door slammed. "Derek. It's your daughter on the phone."

"Which one? I have two daughters," her father snapped back.

What the heck? Is it any wonder I'm still single...for now at least?

"Who is this?" her father shouted, almost causing serious damage to her inner ear.

"Dad, this is your daughter, the private investigator, speaking. Can you tell me where you are?"

"There's no need to be sarcastic, Ruth, your name would have sufficed."

"Sorry, Dad. Your location?"

"I don't know, love."

Ruth placed her hand over the phone and expelled a breath that was filled with annoyance. "Roughly will do. What does your satnav tell you?"

"Why on earth would you ask a stupid question like that?"

"I wasn't aware I had, Dad."

"There are no electrics to the car, and the satnav is built-in, not like the one you have which keeps slipping off your dashboard at inopportune moments."

"And you haven't got a backup one on board?"

"Why would I do a stupid thing like that? Isn't one satnav blooming machine enough for a car?"

"Please don't take your bad mood out on me, Dad, all I'm trying to do here is offer some help. Now work out a solution for me."

"I'm sorry, Ruth. You don't deserve to be on the end of my anger."

"On that, we agree, Dad."

"We passed the village of Erith about a mile ago, at least I think that was the name."

Ruth unclipped her phone from the dashboard and tried to locate the village on Google Maps. "Ah, I have it. Okay, I'm on my way. I'll ring Pat at the garage, see if he can get a breakdown truck out to you ASAP, how's that?"

"Marvellous. Why didn't I think of that?"

"Because, as usual, you've left your brain at home instead of taking it on holiday with you, like most folks do." She chuckled, trying to slice through the strained atmosphere.

"Less of your cheek. You're not too big to put across my knee and give a good hiding, Ruth Morgan."

"I might not be too big, Dad, but there are rules in place for that sort of thing nowadays."

"Phooey! And that's why the kids of today are running riot. No damn discipline any more."

Ruth blew out a breath. "Gotta go, Dad. I'll see you soon. Google is telling me you're around an hour away from me. Make a cup of tea and chill out until I get there. Make it up with Mum, too, while you've got nothing else to do."

"Ha! Some hope of that happening. She's standing here giving me the evil eye as it is. See you soon, and thank you, Ruth."

Ruth ended the call and rang the local garage. One of the other mechanics answered the phone and passed her over to Pat. "Hi, Pat. It's an emergency."

"That's unusual for you, Ruth. What's up?"

"Mum and Dad were on their way to Scotland, and they've broken down. I could do with your help, if you haven't got much on?"

"As long as they're not too far. Where are they?"

"Just north of Erith. I can't give you an accurate location as the electrics have died on the car and Dad couldn't give me any more information than that."

"We'll find him. I can send one of the recovery vehicles out now. You'd better give me your father's mobile number just in case."

"You're a lifesaver. He'll see you right, Pat."

"Always a pleasure to lend a hand when I can."

"You're a treasure. Do me a favour when you rescue them. Tell them off a little for not getting the damn vehicle serviced before they headed off. They won't listen to me. I know nothing, according to my father."

"No problem. I'll wag my finger and tell them that they shouldn't have done such a foolish thing."

Ruth snorted. "That'll tick my dad off if he hears that. I'll let them know you're on your way."

"We might even be able to fix it for them at the location and send them on their way. Hey, what about their breakdown cover? They'd be better off contacting them. Cheaper, too."

"It ran out last month, and yes, I've had a go at them about that."

"Ouch, well, I'm warning you now, my bill won't be cheap."

"Good, it'll teach them a lesson they're not likely to forget in a hurry. Thanks, Pat. I was going to drive out there but I don't see any point in that now."

"Leave it to me to sort out. You get back to your snooping for a living, love."

"You know where I am, if ever I can return the favour." Ruth laughed and ended the call.

She rang her father back and apprised him of the situation and wormed her way out of driving all the way out there to rescue them herself.

With the emergency averted, she turned her attention to Ben and his needs. "Sorry, boy. Let's get our priorities in order and get you sorted."

She drove the couple of miles back to Carmel Cove village green where she opened the door for Ben. He bounded across the soggy grass. She cringed, already regretting her decision, knowing how mucky her car was likely to get once he'd finished. Good job she kept a spare towel in the back of the car for such occasions.

She walked across the green, dodging the muddy potholes as she went. She waved at a couple of the local dog walkers she always managed to stumble across and bid them good morning. Ben was standing at the bottom of an old oak tree, looking up into the branches above and barking at the large grey squirrel that was a frequent escapee in many of his chases.

"Hello, Ruth. How are things with you?"

She was startled by the voice behind her and spun around to find Cynthia, the newest member of the community, standing there. Ruth studied the pained expression on her usually cheerful face. "Hi, sorry. I was miles away. Anything wrong?"

"Not really. I'm feeling a bit out of sorts today. Glad to get out of the house for a while to clear my head. You know how it is."

"Have you had enough of the renovations now?"

Cynthia nodded. "I'd had enough of them at the end of the first week. We're almost six months into them now."

"Gosh, doesn't time fly when you're having fun? Or not in your case. Are you still holed up in that caravan?"

"No. Honestly, it's not as bad as all that. There are plenty of people worse off than me out there. It's just that Reg, in his infinite wisdom, decided to invite his best friend and his wife to visit this coming week-end, and I'm beside myself. Reg keeps assuring me that I'm worrying about nothing, but you know what men are like. The house is full of dust still. The more I clean up, the more I disturb it, only to find it's settled again within a few hours."

"Crikey, Carolyn is in the same situation, and she finished her renovations just before Christmas. Can't you try and dissuade them?"

"Believe me, I've tried. Reg is adamant everything will be hunky-dory by the time they arrive."

"I don't know what else to suggest, Cynthia. I don't envy you in the slightest. You could do without all the hassle at your time of life, no disrespect meant by that."

Cynthia's sad face lit up a little. "None of us are getting any younger, but at sixty-eight, I thought my running around after others was behind me once the children had left home."

Ruth rubbed Cynthia's arm and wracked her brain. "Can you not ring the couple direct? Make them aware of the situation?"

"The Carters are a mixed bag. Callum is henpecked beyond words. He's such a meek and mild-tempered man, as opposed to Belinda— she's an absolute nightmare, the truth be told."

"Sounds like you need different friends," Ruth replied. She shuddered at the thought of playing host to a couple poles apart like that.

"Reg and Callum were in the army together for thirty-odd years. Belinda is Callum's second wife. They've been married for the past seven or eight years, I think it is. Not that it matters." She leaned in close. "I can't stand the woman, and you'll never normally hear those words leave my lips."

"Fancy having to host someone like that. Can't Callum leave her behind and come alone?"

"I don't think that thought has ever occurred to him. I suppose we're just going to have to put up with the blasted woman. Thankfully, they'll only be here for the weekend."

"Is there anything I can do to help you get ready for their visit?" Although she'd offered her services, Ruth was hoping against hope that Cynthia would turn her down. It was her birthday at the weekend, and she had things to prepare back at the cottage for the party James had insisted holding for her special day. All her friends were clubbing together to make it a celebration none of them were likely to forget.

"No, but I really do appreciate the offer. How's trade? Any scandal I should be aware of? Any other dead bodies shown up since that successful author lost her life? I read what happened, that was a terrible incident. I'm so glad your friend got off in the end."

"Nothing coming to mind just yet. Steven was lucky to have me on his side. If I hadn't investigated the case, the local police would have buried the key and forgotten about it for years."

"You're amazing. He's lucky to have such a caring friend as you fighting his corner. Anyway, I'd better get back and start over. Reg is at the local DIY store, picking up a few supplies, new lightbulbs and posh sockets. He wants to change them all over to chrome ones. Anyway, you don't want to hear all my problems. Enjoy the rest of your day. Stay warm in that cosy little office of yours, Ruth."

"Sounds like your life is going to be at breakneck speed for the foreseeable future, Cynthia. Maybe try and persuade your husband that the changes don't have to be made all at the same time, especially when visitors are due."

"That's just it, he's determined to get things looking perfect for when Callum and Belinda arrive. I've told him how ludicrous he's being. He's not listening, as usual, more's the pity."

"Hang in there. The offer still stands. If I can be of any help, just shout."

"You and your wonderful sister and her husband have been far too generous with your time as it is, dear. I can't, no, I won't impose on you further. See you soon, no doubt."

She rattled the poodle's lead and set off. Ben was still barking at his nemesis. She called him; however, he was having far too much fun to obey her command. She strode towards him and attached the lead to his leather collar. "Enough is enough, Ben. Come on, I've got to clean you up before you get in the car."

He panted beside her as they made their way back to the car. She dried his muddy paws and clipped him into his harness in the back seat, then drove to her office where she ran the Carmel Cove Detective

Agency. Once she'd boiled the kettle and added milk and sugar to a mug, she prepared Ben's lunchtime meal of tinned meat and biscuits which he wolfed down within a few minutes. After demolishing his food, he sat beside her and offered his paw.

"What now? Don't tell me you haven't had enough? And no, you're not having a treat. You still have a few kilos to lose until the vet is happy with you."

Ben hung his head in shame and slipped under the desk. Despite having a comfy bed to rest in, he always preferred being close to her during the day. The phone rang.

"Hello, Carmel Cove Detective Agency. How can I help?"

"Help! Someone has run off with my gerbil, and I need you to track them down and put them in prison for trying to fence stolen goods."

She leaned back in her chair and let out a laugh. "Steven Swanson, how dare you keep ringing me up, making these preposterous allegations?"

"Who else am I going to ring to brighten my day? How are you, stranger?"

"Stranger? We only met at am-dram on Sunday. May I remind you that was only four days ago?"

"Blimey, is it that long already? No wonder I'm missing you."

Ruth smiled. It was wonderful to hear him so happy. It had taken him a good few weeks to get over his traumatic ordeal of being banged up in a police cell, when Inspector Littlejohn had accused him of killing one of his idols. However, the rest of the amateur dramatic club they belonged to had done everything they could think of to make the transition back to normal life an easy one. He was an inspiration to everyone, very talented with his set designs, which had been the cause of his recent problems. Steven was also the caretaker at the local school. How he managed to fit everything in confounded her. "You're incorrigible. What can I do for you?"

"In other words, get to the point, I'm busy, right?"

"Actually, for once, I'm not. My desk and diary are clear for the foreseeable future. Now that isn't going to help pay my bills, is it?"

"Crikey, a top-notch investigator like you with no work on your hands? Are people mad? Want me to go out and commit a crime and leave a few clues dotted around for you? Would that help?"

Ruth roared. "Don't, you'll have me splitting my sides soon. I'm glad you haven't lost your sense of humour, matey."

"I'll admit there are days when I sit back and reflect on how close I came to losing my freedom. I'll forever be in your debt, Ruth."

Unexpected tears welled up, and she swallowed down the large lump that had formed in her throat. "I couldn't *not* help you, Steven. You're one of my dearest friends and didn't deserve to be treated that way by the police, and Littlejohn in particular. Still, we need to move on from that. We have so much coming up to look forward to, like my party for instance."

"How could I forget that? That's why I'm calling really, to try and persuade you to dress up for the night."

"By that I take it you want me to wear one of those god-awful dresses other women seem to favour wearing? No way, is my response to that. The last time I wore one of your dresses was on that fateful night. Even if I didn't loathe the things before, I definitely do now. I'm happier in trousers, you know that."

"It's just I've been saving this special dress, especially for you. Won't you reconsider, Ruthie Baby?"

She sniggered. Even using the cute name he only ever used for her wouldn't be enough to change her mind. "One word: not-in-a-million-years."

"Something wrong with your maths there, Ruth. I think you'll find that's five words."

"Stop splitting hairs. What else can I help you with today?"

"Charming. Are you trying to get rid of me by any chance?"

"Never. I wouldn't dream of it."

"Okay, we need to make arrangements for Saturday. I've been tidying up the community centre after work every night and I have to say I'm delighted with the results so far."

Ruth groaned. "I hope you haven't gone to too much trouble on my account? It's only another candle on the cake. Soon there won't be any more room on the damn thing."

"Nonsense. Thirty-six isn't old. You're in the prime of your life."

"If you say so. There are some days I feel a darn sight older." Her mobile rang. "Hang on a sec, Mum's on the other line. I'd better get it otherwise she'll freak out."

"I'm not going anywhere."

Ruth answered the call. "Hi, Mum. How's it going?"

"Fine. Just ringing up to say we're on our way again, dear. It was something technical at fault. The damn thing needed some form of update. Well, it's all beyond me. Whoever heard of a car needing to be updated like one of those ruddy computers? Anyway, letting you know that we're up and running again. Thank you for being you and coming to our rescue, not for the first time."

Ruth smiled. She knew her mother was happy again because of the way she was chuntering on. "My pleasure as always, Mum. Have a fabulous holiday."

"We will. See you next week."

Ruth should have been upset with her parents for going away when her birthday was imminent, but in truth, she was grateful not to have her mother fussing around her on her big day. She wasn't the best organiser in the world and tended to panic at the drop of a hat. Ruth ended the call and picked up the office phone again. "Hi, I'm here."

"What was that all about?" Steven enquired.

"They broke down, and I had to get Pat to rescue them. They tend to self-implode when anything like that happens."

"Ah, Ruthie Baby to the rescue yet again. You do so much good for so many people, you've definitely earned your angel's wings."

"I doubt that. I'm hardly a goody two-shoes."

"Not far off it. Anyway, going back to Saturday… Oh, and I have to say this, please or offend, I can't believe your parents won't be around to celebrate your birthday. Did they forget?"

"Nope, honestly, I'm fine with it. Let them enjoy themselves. They've worked really hard over the years. I don't blame them for taking off when time permits. We all know how short this life is."

"You're amazing. Kind, considerate, and a simply wonderful

friend. Oh gosh, I'm in tears here. We'll make this a special birthday, one you're never going to forget."

"Sounds ominous. I hope it goes off without a hitch. What with all the drama I've experienced in the past few months, it's nice to get a breather now and again."

"Famous last words, coming from a private investigator. Oh well, I'd better crack on, love. It was nice catching up, and if you change your mind about the dress, let me know. It's stunning, even tempted to wear it myself."

"Ha, don't let me stand in your way. Speak soon."

"I might just do that and make a surprise entrance. That'll have you eating your words or spitting out your birthday cake." His laughter filled the line before he hung up.

She was left smiling, recapping the conversation they'd had. She wouldn't put it past Steven to do something as outrageous as that.

Ruth spent the rest of the day tinkering with her website and creating a batch of new flyers for her business. She finally got fed up with the loneliness and locked up the office. After stopping off at the park to let Ben have a quick run around, she went home. James was in the kitchen when she arrived. She crept up behind him and wrapped her arms around his waist, startling him.

He turned in her arms, and they shared a welcome embrace.

"Hey, you. I've missed you," he said, lightly kissing the top of her head.

"Ditto. It's been a long day, one that I'd rather forget."

"Still no work?"

"Not even a 'Help, my pussy is missing!'" She smiled up at him.

He pecked the tip of her nose. "Well, that doesn't bode well for the future, Ruth. What are you going to do about it?"

"Steven suggested he go out and commit some crimes and leave some clues dotted around for me to follow. I talked him out of doing that, though."

"Thank goodness. Well, we're as busy as ever down at the station. Not what you wanted to hear, I'm guessing?"

She ran a hand through his blond hair and tugged it a little. "Nope, not what I wanted to hear at all, buster. How's my archenemy?"

"She sends her regards."

Ruth took a step back and narrowed her eyes. "Really?"

"Nope, just teasing. In all fairness, I do think she's mellowed a little since the last case you worked on."

"Let's face it, she couldn't get any blooming worse. I'm glad she's backed off from laying into you because of your association with me."

"I'm a big boy, I can look after myself, although even her death stares were beginning to chip away at me. Shame you're not doing so well at the moment. I was hoping to chuck in my job and come and work for you in the near future."

She removed herself from his grasp and walked across the room to the fridge. She poured two glasses of white wine and returned the bottle. "It's getting desperate, love. Only just about keeping my head above water, if you must know."

He tutted and shook his head. "We both know why that is, don't we?"

"Don't say it. I can do without another lecture about me doing work pro bono. In my defence, my last two cases have been for two dear friends desperate for my help."

He approached her and slung an arm around her shoulder. "Free work doesn't pay the bills, darling."

"I realise that. Don't tell me you would have charged them when they were both at their lowest ebb?"

He nodded. "Yep. Your efforts deserve to be paid for. You need to take a step back now and again and realise what you're worth. You put a thousand percent into that business of yours and need to be rewarded financially for it."

"Please, James, I don't want to fall out about this. I need to run my business how I see fit. I'm not one of life's money-grabbers. I like to give back where I can. Yes, sometimes that turns out to be to the detriment of my financial wealth, but it makes me feel good about myself."

He sipped at his wine and considered his reply. "I would never stand in your way, Ruth. However, giving your time and expertise away for free…"

"I know, I know…doesn't pay the bills or put money in my bank account."

Sensing they were going around in circles, she quickly changed the subject. "Steven rang today, tried his darnedest to get me to change my mind about wearing a dress on Saturday."

"I'm in agreement with him. You always look stunning in a dress and yet you're too stubborn to wear one." He stepped closer and glanced down at her long slender legs. "Those pins of yours need showing off."

She placed a hand to his cheek. "Most people would be envious in your position, the only one privy to seeing what I have hiding beneath my trousers."

He bent down and gave her a kiss that took her breath away. "If you put it like that, it suits me. Did Steven say how the party preparations are coming along? Does he want me to pop in and lend him a hand?"

"He said he's almost done. Even if you offered, I don't think he'd accept your help, James. He's such a control freak."

"He's a diva." They both laughed. "Don't tell him I said that."

"He'd probably see it as a compliment, knowing him. I'm so grateful to you all for arranging this. It's just another birthday really, not even a special one."

"Everyone in the community wanted to give back for the efforts you've put in to help a few of the residents recently. Shame they didn't just put their hands in their pockets and raise some funds for you instead," he added, sounding a little disgruntled.

"Don't be bitter, love. I'm just grateful they thought of me."

"I suppose. Ignore me, I'm becoming a grumpy old man."

She smiled. "Never. You're just looking out for me, which I appreciate more than you know. Fancy watching a film tonight?"

"I recorded that James Bond film at the weekend."

"Depends who is playing Bond. You know how much I detest that Daniel Craig. He has as much charisma as you have in your little finger. All the other Bonds have managed to set my heart fluttering. Not him. Every time I see him on the screen, I'm tempted to run to the loo and empty my stomach."

"Wow, really? You must be in a minority then. The women at work all drool over him."

"More fool them."

"Anyway, it's that Pierce Brosnan in *Die Another Day.*"

"I can't remember that one. I'm up for it. I'll grab some crisps and chocolate. We can pretend we're at the cinema."

"Nutter. That's why I love you, you never stay down for long."

She tilted her head. "I wasn't aware that I was down."

"Okay, my mistake. Let's not get into an argument and spoil the evening."

"Agreed. You set up the film, and I'll gather all the treats together."

They spent several hours cuddled up on the sofa, with Ben scrunched up on the end beside Ruth, not wishing to miss out at all. The film was one of the better Bond movies she'd seen, and Pierce did what he set out to do: had her heart fluttering every time he spoke.

2

he next couple of days panned out to be the same for Ruth and consisted of her either sitting at her desk, staring at the phone, willing it to ring, or taking Ben out for a long walk to break up the monotony. Times were becoming desperate now. If work didn't pick up soon, she'd be forced to jack in the detective agency and turn her attention to finding 'a proper job', as her mother would say.

She'd come into the office first thing on Saturday to put away the files she'd been forced to tidy up to kill time the previous day, in spite of it being her birthday. James was on duty anyway until three, so there was little point staying at home.

Around midday, she took Ben for a windswept walk in the park where she met up with Cynthia and her poodle, Roxy. "Hey, Cynthia, how are things going? Are you out escaping your dreaded visitors?"

Her new friend chuckled. "How did you guess? Belinda is being a damned nightmare, and she only arrived last night. I decided to excuse myself and bring Roxy out."

"That's so sad for you to feel uncomfortable in your own home like that."

She shrugged. "It is what it is. I refuse to stand in Reg's way. He has every right to have his friends come and stay, and I'll do my best to play hostess to them to keep the peace but…"

"But?" Ruth slipped her arm through Cynthia's as they walked.

Roxy and Ben ran around them barking and play-growling at each other.

"Well, everyone has their limit in this world. I think I've reached mine already. I have at least another forty-eight hours to contend with. It's her damn voice I can't abide. It sets my teeth on edge every time she speaks, and that's frequently, unfortunately. Why couldn't Callum find a woman who doesn't like the sound of her own voice? It's a high-pitched squeak. I swear it's put on most of the time, that's how it comes across to me."

"She sounds a nightmare. I feel for you, sweetheart."

Cynthia patted her hand. "Enough about my woes. Hey, didn't I hear on the grapevine that it's a certain private investigator's birthday today?"

"It might be. Sorry, I never thought to invite you to the soiree we're having at the community centre this evening. I'm sure we could find a spare table for you if you're desperate to get away from your annoying guest for a few hours."

Cynthia chuckled. "That's very sweet of you. I think she's the type to take offence if I spent too much time away from the house during their visit. She looked daggers at me when I announced I was taking Roxy for her walk. Anyway, enough about her, I have a little some-thing for you, just in case I met you down here this morning." From her bag she plucked a small package which was attached to an envelope.

Ruth was taken aback by the gesture, and tears moistened her eyes. She swiped them away with her gloved hands. "That's so kind of you. You really shouldn't have."

"Nonsense. You've been a wonderful friend to me since our arrival. It's only something small. I hope you like it."

Ruth struggled to remove the Sellotape from the package with her gloves on, so she slipped them off. Once she'd torn off the paper and opened the box that had been revealed, she gasped. "My goodness, it's beautiful, Cynthia. You shouldn't be spending this amount of money on me."

"Nonsense, I'm glad you like it. The green stone will look perfect against your red hair."

Ruth shook her head in disbelief. The silver chain set off the green onyx stone beautifully. "I can't thank you enough. It truly is one of the nicest gifts I've ever received. You're very generous. I'll treasure it and wear it this evening."

Cynthia smiled warmly. "I'm thrilled you love it so much. Well, I hate to run out on you like this but I'd better get back to the house before they send out a search party for me."

Ruth leaned forward and kissed her friend on the cheek. "Thank you so much. Listen, if things get too fraught for you, give me a ring or just drop by the house. Obviously, we'll be out this evening but we'll probably resurface around ten tomorrow morning."

"Don't you worry your pretty head about me, I'll be fine. Have a wonderful evening. You do so much for others, take time out to have fun at your party."

"Thank you again for the wonderful necklace. Try to enjoy the rest of your day, lovely lady."

Cynthia called Roxy to join her and set off back to her car. Her shoulders slumped, and Ruth's heart went out to her.

"Ben, come on, boy. Playtime is over. We should go and get ready for the party now."

She arrived home and got on the phone straight away. One by one, Ruth rang every member of the am-dram club to see how they were going with their tasks for the party. Everyone bar Hilary answered the phone. Knowing Hilary the way she did, Ruth wasn't too concerned. Hils was the type who couldn't concentrate on doing more than one thing at a time. She should have been born a man really. Ruth sniggered at the thought.

The others had assured her that everything was on course and the evening would be perfect, there was nothing for her to worry about.

Except she would. Ruth spent her life arranging things for others. She hated being on the receiving end of other people's generosity.

James came home while she was having a long soak in the bath. He stood in the doorway and whistled. "No one looks more stunning in this world than you, Ruth Morgan, soon-to-be Winchester."

She laughed. "You could be biased in your opinion. Want to join me?"

He didn't need telling twice. He stripped off, stepped over Ben who was lying beside the bath and got in.

They often shared a bath together, sounding off after the fraught day they'd individually had.

"How was work?" Ruth asked.

"Same as always. Mundane at the best of times. No new cases to report. How has your birthday been so far?"

"Wonderful. I met Cynthia at the park. She gave me a beautiful necklace. I promised to wear it this evening."

"Is she coming? I don't recall her name being on the list."

"No. I forgot about inviting her; however, I think she would have declined anyway because she has 'friends'—I use the word loosely —visiting."

"Sounds cryptic. Care to enlighten me?"

"They're more her husband's friends. She was down at the park escaping the woman's cringing voice."

"Wow, does that type of thing still go on? If I invited someone to stay who you didn't like, you'd take off for the weekend rather than have to play hostess with the mostest, right?"

Ruth tipped back her head and laughed. "You're not wrong there. I don't suffer fools gladly, do I? Luckily, I get on well with all your friends and their other halves. I'm going to get out now. The last thing I want to do is turn up looking like an old prune. Stay and enjoy."

She leaned over and kissed him. "Are you sure I can't tempt you to stay?"

"Nope. I've been in here an hour as it is. Have fun."

His mouth turned down at the sides. "I'll be out soon."

"There's no need. We've got at least three hours to go before we have to leave."

*T*he hours swiftly flew by. They both fussed over Ben for a little while and then decided to get changed into their birthday bash clothes. Ruth had chosen a smart white trouser suit and a mint green T-shirt-styled top underneath. It wasn't her intention to wear the top initially, but she felt it would set off her necklace beautifully. When she saw James dressed in his Tuxedo her heart raced.

"Don't we make a smart couple?" she asked, sidling up to him.

He pecked her on the lips. "You'll be the most beautiful woman there tonight."

"You say the sweetest things."

James opened the drawer in the chest beside him and extracted a package.

"What's this? I thought we'd agreed no extravagant presents for our birthdays this year?" She scowled at him for breaking his promise.

"I know. It's only a little something. I just wanted to show my appreciation for you being such a wonderful person and for finally becoming my fiancée, even though we haven't set a date for the wedding yet. Don't roll your eyes at me, I'm not pressurising you to do that...yet. It's a small gift to show how much I love you and to thank you for being such a pivotal part of my life. I'd be lost without you."

Tears dripped onto her cheek. "Damn, look what you've made me do now. I'll have to redo my makeup in a second. What is it? And before I open it, you're the sweetest man ever to step foot on this earth, James. I love our life together and spending each day with you. I wouldn't have it any other way."

"Good, because I feel the same about you. Open it."

She tore open the gift to reveal a silver set of earrings that had a green onyx in each setting. "Oh my God, did you and Cynthia collaborate on this or is it a mere coincidence?"

"Purely coincidental, I assure you. What are the odds on that?"

"A billion to one, I'm guessing. They're beautiful. I'll wear them this evening. Thank you so much, James. I'll treasure them."

"I know you will. Right, it's time we were leaving. Well, after you've touched up your makeup. I'll put Ben in the garden, give you some space. Happy birthday, darling."

They shared a kiss, then James left her doing the repairs to her face. Five minutes later, Ruth exited the bedroom and went to find James who was standing by the back door. Once Ben had been fed and settled in his bed, they put on their winter coats and left the house. They'd decided to walk to the community centre that evening; there was no rain forecast, although the breeze was still whipping around them. They stopped off at her sister's house, to pick up Carolyn and her family. Keith was still wearing the bandage from his mishap a few months back, and the boys, Ian and Robin, seemed as high-spirited as usual. All of them were dressed smartly, which pleased Ruth. Not everyone put in the effort to look nice on special occasions these days.

They arrived at the community centre at the proposed time: seven-thirty on the dot. Not a moment sooner or later as instructed by Steven. The second Ruth stepped through the door, the room erupted with everyone cheering, and the band struck up *Happy Birthday* which everyone sang along to. Ruth's cheeks heated up.

Steven rushed towards her and hugged her. "You look stunning, I have to admit that. Well, you will do once you get out of that damned coat of yours." He tore the garment from her and gathered the rest of the family's coats which he whisked away. Then he rejoined them and requested they accompany him on a tour of the room.

Everyone else was eager to see Ruth to wish her happy birthday, but they probably knew they wouldn't stand a chance of getting to her until Steven had finished his tour. The food laid out on the trestle tables was outstanding and looked thoroughly professional. Ruth felt extremely proud and honoured that her friends had put so much effort into the display for her benefit. She was the luckiest woman alive.

Each of her am-dram associates came up and squeezed her tightly. "I can't thank all of you enough for doing this for little ol' me. Your kindness is overwhelming."

"You're worth the effort and the extra hours we've had to work this week," Gemma announced.

"Thank you, Gemma. When can we tuck in? I'm starving."

Steven clapped to gain the room's attention. "The guest of honour has spoken, or at least her stomach has. Dig in, folks, form an orderly queue behind Ruth and her wonderful family. Let the festivities begin."

Ruth latched on to his arm and pulled him in for a hug. "You're amazing. The best friend a girl could wish to have."

He took a step back, tears brimming his eyes. "You're the amazing one. Everyone thinks the world of you, sweetheart. This is our way of giving back for having you in our lives. I love you lots, Ruthie Baby. Now, enjoy yourself."

She kissed him and swallowed down the lump bulging in her throat.

The band started up, playing soft music until all the food, or at least most of it, had been consumed. Then the tempo changed, and everyone hit the dance floor. The next half an hour consisted of Ruth standing in the centre as her friends and neighbours danced around her. Just for the evening, her community made her feel important. She had rarely felt such emotions.

"It's a shame Mum and Dad couldn't be here," Carolyn shouted beside her.

Ruth shrugged. "Honestly, it truly doesn't matter to me. As long as they're out there enjoying themselves, that's what counts."

"Your friends think the world of you, Ruth, that much is evident. You're a very lucky lady indeed."

She nodded and smiled. "I am."

Around eight-thirty her mobile rang. She was in the middle of doing the twist with her nephews and only just managed to hear it. Thinking it was her parents, she stepped outside to take the call. She was wrong...

"Ruth, it's Cynthia. I'm so sorry to call you on your special day. I'm beside myself and I didn't know who to turn to for help."

"Calm down, Cynthia. What's wrong? You know I'm always available to take your call."

"It's Callum. He's gone missing?"

"Your guest? When?"

"It's been a few hours now. I left it as long as I could but now I'm terrified something has happened to him. And before you ask, yes, we've tried ringing his mobile, but there's no answer."

"Don't worry. I'll be there in a little while."

"No! Please, I didn't want you to leave your party. Please, tell me what we should do. I've rung the police—they're refusing to help as he's only been gone a few hours. They told me a person has to be missing twenty-four hours before they're prepared to do anything to help us."

"That's right. I don't mind coming over to help out, honestly."

"I don't want you to do that. I'm probably being foolish, love. I shouldn't have rung you. Go back to your party, we'll go out and search for him. Sorry."

With that, the line went dead. Ruth glanced up at the stars twinkling.

"What's going on?" James asked, startling her. "Was it your parents?"

"No. It was Cynthia. She's concerned about her guest. He's gone missing, and she wanted some advice on what to do next."

James wagged his finger. "I know that look. You're not leaving your own party, Ruth. I refuse to let you do it."

"But, James. She needs my help. You didn't hear how desperate she sounded."

"There's nothing anyone can do, Ruth. He's in a strange town. Let's face it, Carmel Cove isn't that big. He'll find his way home soon. Come on, I was enjoying my dance with you."

He grabbed her hand and pulled her back inside and onto the dance floor. Although she drifted through the rest of the evening, appearing to those around her as if she was having a blast, Ruth found herself distracted by Cynthia's call and had to resist the temptation to ring her back several times.

"Don't think I don't know what's going on in that pretty head of yours," James whispered in her ear during the final dance of the evening.

"I'm allowed to be concerned about a friend, James. There's no law against that, is there?"

"Don't snap at me. Geez, Ruth, let it go for one evening, will you? Enjoy yourself for a change without the distraction of work."

"That's a tad harsh, even for you. I have enjoyed myself. I *am* enjoying myself."

His arms tightened around her as they swayed to the sound of Lionel Richie's *Hello*. "The community has done you proud tonight. Everything has gone according to plan—"

"In other words, you're telling me not to spoil it?" she interrupted him.

"I didn't say that. God, you can be so annoying at times," he bit back through gritted teeth.

"I'm sorry. My mind is elsewhere, James. Can we go home now?"

He dropped his arms and shrugged. "Why not? That was the last dance. The others will be disappointed to see you leave before the end."

"They'll be fine once I explain the situation to them, although I have no intention of doing that this evening. Can you grab our coats while I make our excuses to Steven?"

"Good luck. I have a feeling he's going to be livid with you."

She grinned. "He'll be putty in my hand, he always is." However, when she wandered across to where Steven was standing at the bar with a couple of their friends, he was far from happy.

"What? Is this one of your wind-ups? It's barely eleven, and you're calling it a night? I thought we could go on to a nightclub, to dance until the early hours. It's your birthday, and you're chucking in the towel early."

Ruth sighed and patted his forearm. "I'm worn out, love. I'm sorry, it's not that I don't appreciate it. I'll see you all back here at seven tomorrow, how's that? Thank you for making this such a fabulous evening."

"If I can't persuade the guest of honour then we might as well ditch our plans," Steven announced to the rest of the group around them.

There were a few jeers, but in the main, the others accepted the situation for what it was and bid Ruth goodnight with a hug and a kiss.

She left the community centre feeling strangely emotional and struggled to put a finger on why that was. She shuddered as the cold evening air seeped into her bones on the walk home. James even removed his coat and placed it around her shoulders; however, his gallant gesture did nothing to dispel her discomfort. She regretted not bringing the car with them that evening, for two reasons: firstly, it would have protected them from the chill, and secondly, it would have meant that they could have dropped by Cynthia's on the way back to the cottage to see if Callum had turned up from his adventure.

Ben greeted them, his tail mimicking a helicopter's blades. After removing her coat, she got down on her knees to stroke him, nuzzling the fur around his neck. He moaned softly, relishing the affection. "I missed you this evening, boy. Have you been good?"

"Seriously? What do you expect him to say in response to that, Ruth?" James tutted and removed a couple of glasses from the cupboard.

"Just stop it! I know what this is all about. Don't spoil my birthday, James, please."

He turned around swiftly. His arm caught one of the glasses and sent it tumbling to the floor where it smashed into tiny pieces.

"Now look what you've done," she shouted at him and rushed to get the dustpan and brush before Ben cut a paw on the shards of glass littered across the floor.

"You clear it up, I've had it for the evening. I'll take my drink up to bed. I'll be in the spare room, in case you're wondering."

"I wasn't. You're being childish, James."

"Whatever. It's still a few minutes to midnight. Enjoy the rest of your birthday. We tried to do our best to make it a night to remember for you, and failed miserably, apparently."

Ruth knew there was little point in arguing with him so kept quiet and continued to sweep up the mess he'd made. He kicked the chair on his way out of the room. She couldn't tell if that was by mistake or intentional. Either way, she cringed. She hated falling out with him and had a problem fathoming out how the evening had developed into them detesting being in the same room as each other.

She looked over at Ben who was curled up in his bed, staring at her with his soulful eyes. He hated any form of conflict, too. Once she'd completed her task, she patted her leg and called him to her. He padded across the floor and sat in front of her. She flung her arms around him and let the tears of frustration finally break free.

Why don't people understand my need to help the community and its inhabitants? None of this is about servicing my own needs or requirements. All I'm guilty of is trying to help others. My birthday doesn't matter in the grand scheme of things, my parents have proven that.

"That's a bit OTT, Ruth," she reprimanded herself. "Do you want to go in the garden, Ben?"

He rushed towards the back door. She let him out ahead of her and wrapped the broken glass in some newspaper then placed it in the recycle bin near the back door. She hurried inside again to shelter from the rain that was now falling. "Ben, hurry up, boy."

Ben stopped at the back door until she invited him to step on the towel. Taking another towel from the pile in the corner that she kept especially for drying him, she ran it down the length of his right side first then said, "Turn around, boy."

Ben did as instructed, making a mockery of what James had said about the dog not understanding her. The more you spoke to your four-legged friends, the more they understood. He was an exceptional dog, in her eyes anyway.

Ruth poured herself a brandy, fearing if she didn't, she'd be in for a long night, her mind whirring out of control, worried about Cynthia's friend. She secured the back door and placed the chain on the front one then went upstairs to bed with Ben close on her heels. She wasn't surprised to find the bed empty, although the fact James had followed through on his threat upset her. She shrugged and closed the door quietly. "Guess who's going to be sleeping with me tonight?"

Ben ran to the bed and made himself comfortable at the bottom. He watched her move around the room for a few moments until his eyes became heavy and he drifted off to sleep. Ruth removed her makeup, carried out the rest of her nightly routine and slipped under the duvet. She shivered against the chill, but sipping at her brandy helped her insides to glow. She managed to drift off to sleep soon after.

3

*"C*an I come in?" James asked, poking his head around the bedroom door.

Ruth stretched out the knots in her back and lifted her head to look at him. "You can as long as you don't have a go at me."

His chin dropped to his chest, and he entered, waving a white towel. "Truce? I'm sorry for snapping at you last night. You're your own person, Ruth, I shouldn't interfere with the way you want to run your life."

"Run my life?" She propped up the pillows behind her and pressed her back into them. "Not sure where that's coming from, James. All I'm trying to do is help a friend out. Yes, maybe that was at the expense of me enjoying my own birthday party, but it was my choice. Did you hear me complaining about it? No, then why should you and the others? It's not that I didn't appreciate the way everyone rallied around to put on a fantastic party for me, but in my heart of hearts, it's hard for me to enjoy myself when a friend of mine is suffering, going out of their minds with worry. Surely you can understand that, can't you?"

He sat on the bed beside her and grasped her hand. He kissed it and smiled. "I'm sorry. Can we blame it on the devil drink?"

She shrugged and pulled her mouth down at the sides. "All the devil drink does is loosen your tongue to reveal what you're truly thinking."

He shook his head. "That's grossly unfair, Ruth, and you know it is."

"I know nothing of the sort. Anyway, I don't want to start the day the way we ended yesterday. I need to get up and haul my backside over to Cynthia's right away." She threw back the cover.

"Oi, give me a chance to get out of the way first. Do you want me to come with you?"

"I'd hate to force you to do anything you didn't want to do."

He stood and held a hand out in front of him. "Stop this. I've apologised. Let that be the end of it. It's my day off work, or supposed to be, but I'm willing to spend the day out there searching for this bloke, if that's what you want. Do you?"

They stood twelve inches apart.

She peered through blue eyes to his soul. "If that's what you truly want to do, then yes, you can tag along and help out. The choice is yours," she replied, a nonchalant edge to her tone. She bit down on her tongue.

He ran a hand across the exasperated expression etched into his handsome features. "Or, I could stay here and clean up the house and fix the Sunday roast like I usually do on my day off."

"Ouch! Was that another dig at me?"

"No, it actually wasn't. Blooming heck, Ruth, drop it before you do some real damage to our relationship, will you?"

She scratched the nape of her neck and mumbled an apology of her own. "Okay, I'm sorry. Come with me if you like…"

"Why do I sense a 'but' coming here?"

"Not at all. But, you need to let me get on with my work and not interfere in an official capacity."

He pointed at her and laughed. "You don't even realise when you say the word. All right, you win, I promise. The first sign of me stepping on your toes, and you have my permission to tell me to bog off."

She held her clenched fist out for him to bump. "Deal. Now, I need to jump in the shower. Be a love and let Ben out in the garden, will you?"

"Glad to see I still have my uses," he replied with a smirk.

"When you're not in a strop and storming off to the spare room."

He shook his head and beckoned Ben to leave the room with him. Ben hesitated for a moment until Ruth nodded at him. He scooted off the bed and followed James downstairs. Ruth studied herself in the mirror. Her skin appeared dry and wrinkled from the drink she'd consumed the previous evening. She'd have to counter that with lots of water today. Still, that was the least of her worries. She needed to get a wriggle on and get over to Cynthia's. Turning on the tap drowned everything out until she'd showered and dried herself. She entered the bedroom to find James sitting on the bed, a tray of breakfast goodies beside him.

"Wow, you did all this for me?"

"Yep, to prove how much I love you."

"I never doubted that, James." The phone rang, and she crossed the room to answer it. "Hello."

"Oh, thank goodness you're awake. I thought I might be ringing you too early. I'm not, am I, Ruth? Oh dear, sorry, I should have said, this is Cynthia."

Ruth chuckled. "It's not too early. I was about to eat breakfast and then drop over to see you. Has your friend returned yet?"

"No. We're going out of our minds. None of us have slept well at all. Would you mind coming to see us? Taking on the case, Ruth? Of course, we'll pay the going rate. Money doesn't matter to us. Callum's safe return is what is important."

"Don't worry, James has promised to help me look for him today. We'll be with you in half an hour, how's that?"

"Wonderful. We'll do our best not to stress out too much in the meantime."

"See you soon, Cynthia." Ruth ended the call and plonked down on the bed beside James. "They're worried sick. I hope we can locate Callum soon. You'll be pleased to know that Cynthia mentioned paying for my services."

He grinned and tore off a piece of toast with his teeth. "Yay, I'm glad at least one of your friends has decided your hard work is worth paying for."

"Are you having a shower?" she asked, choosing to ignore his latest dig.

"Yep, it won't take me long. I'm starving and intend eating my breakfast first, if that's all right with you?"

"It is. Just be quick about it." Ruth left her breakfast and swiftly got dressed, pulling on a pair of faithful jeans, a T-shirt and a big woolly jumper, aware that they would need to be out there, facing what the elements intended throwing at them.

"Eat before it goes cold, or I'll never cook for you again."

She tutted and bit into her cool, crispy toast and marmalade. "It's still warm. Thanks, James."

"One of these days your nose is going to grow as long as Pinocchio's and stay that way."

She grinned. "Shoo…we need to get moving soon."

*T*hey left the house, taking Ben with them, and twenty-five minutes later Ruth was knocking on the door of the Old Station House. She let out an exhausted breath. "Only just made it. I'm trying to brush up on my timekeeping skills, in case that's what has put people off contacting me."

James laughed. "You're an odd one."

"Not odd at all."

Cynthia looked terrible when she opened the door. She clearly hadn't slept at all through the night. She gestured for them to enter the house and hugged them both, tears brimming her already red, sore eyes. "I'm so glad you're willing to take the case on, Ruth, I'll be forever in your debt."

"Why don't we join the others and you can run through what happened?"

"They're in the lounge. None of us have slept all night. I wanted to go out there and look for him, but the others warned me against that in case anyone else slipped off the face of the earth, too. There's no reason for him to just disappear like this, Ruth." Her voice was high with anxiety.

Ruth rubbed Cynthia's arm to try to calm her down. "Let's wait until we're with the others, love. Are they in here?" Ruth pointed at the room she knew to be the lounge.

"Yes, go through. I'll go and make us all a drink."

"Thanks, coffee for us."

Cynthia veered off towards the kitchen at the back of the property and left Ruth and James to enter the lounge by themselves. Cynthia's husband appeared relieved to see them, and the other person in the room, she took to be Belinda, stared at Ruth, studying her through a narrowed gaze.

"Hi, I'm Ruth, and this is my fiancé, James."

"Are you going to be the ones who find him?" Belinda asked, her voice faltering a little. She took another tissue from the box on the table in front of her and dabbed at her dripping nose.

"I hope so. We're definitely going to try our best."

"Well? Aren't you going to ask any questions? Isn't that what you're supposed to do in circumstances such as this?"

"Give the girl a chance, Belinda," Reg snapped, rolling his eyes up to the low ceiling.

"I'll wait until Cynthia joins us, it'll save me having to repeat myself, if that's all right with you, Belinda?"

She waved a hand in front of her. "Do what you want. In case you're all forgetting, it's my husband who has been reported missing. Clearly that doesn't mean anything." Her voice squeaked, annoyingly, just as Cynthia had warned her.

"Of course it does," James piped up. "I'm sure Cynthia won't be too long."

"Have some patience, Belinda, for goodness' sake. You need to wait and give the girl a chance," Reg repeated, harshly.

"Wait? Did you just say the W-word? I've been *waiting* all blooming night to get this investigation started..." Belinda complained.

"Exactly. A few more minutes won't harm you," Reg stated, cutting Belinda off.

Ruth cringed at the atmosphere in the room. She was tempted to leave and go in search of Cynthia but decided to stay put when the lounge door sprang open and her friend entered. James quickly jumped to his feet to help her with the tray.

"Let me take that from you."

"You're very kind, James. Place it on the table, and I'll distribute the cups from there." They waited patiently, some more patient than others, for Cynthia to hand around the china cups and saucers. "Okay, how far have you got?" she asked Ruth.

"We haven't. We've been waiting for you," Ruth replied, taking a sip from her cup and placing it on the small side table next to her seat on the couch. "Now, why don't you start at the beginning? Who wants to go first?"

"Me," Belinda shouted. "I'm the one who was out with him last night. These two weren't."

The more Ruth interacted with the woman, the more she disliked her for some reason. "Makes sense. What time did you set off?"

"We were fed up of being cramped up in here all afternoon. I came here to see the views, after all, not to be stuck inside all the time," Belinda said unkindly.

"I'm sorry. That's my fault," Reg apologised, his head dipping as if he were a child who'd been scolded by the headmistress.

"Can we stop with the blame game? No one is to *blame*. If you'll just stick to the facts, Belinda, we'll get this done a whole lot quicker, which will enable us to begin our search. You were saying?" Ruth admonished the woman who appeared to be intent on adding to the already oppressive atmosphere.

"We took a stroll, to stretch our legs. Callum fancied a drink in the coffee shop on the edge of town. We stopped there for a pot of tea, after which we decided to walk the length of the high street. It didn't take long, as you can imagine. Why anyone would choose to live in this dump is beyond me."

"The facts," Ruth reminded the obtuse woman.

"Callum was a bit antsy all day yesterday, wasn't he, Reg and Cynthia?"

"I wouldn't say that," Reg replied offhandedly.

"Neither would I," Cynthia agreed.

Ruth glanced at her friends when they spoke and then back at Belinda. "Antsy? What do you mean by that? In what way?"

"Goodness me, it seems you two didn't really know Callum at all if you didn't pick up on his foul mood. I can assure you, he wasn't himself at all. There was something bothering him, that's why I suggested going out to stretch our legs. I tried to get out of him what was wrong, but he was having none of it. Clammed up, he did."

"Okay, that's strange. So after you had a drink and walked the length of the high street, what happened next?" Ruth took a sip of her coffee.

Belinda sighed and stared down at the carpet in front of her. "He was annoying me. I was furious that he wasn't speaking to me. We argued, and he told me to get lost." She sniffled and wiped her nose on a tissue. "No one speaks to me like that and gets away with it. I slapped him and stormed off in the opposite direction. I told him I would see him back here. Except he never came back, and now he's missing. You should be out there looking for him, not grilling me about the whys and wherefores that went on." Her harsh exterior crumbled, and she sobbed.

If it was anyone else she was dealing with, Ruth would have felt sorry for them; however, she had taken an instant dislike to Belinda, which was unusual for her. Maybe her judgement of the newcomer had been clouded by what Cynthia had said about her at the park. She tried to shake off the feeling and be professional when she spoke to her again. "We'll get out there when we've been given all the facts, Belinda, and not before."

The woman's head rose slowly, and her eyes narrowed. "Meaning what? I can tell by the way you said that you don't believe me."

Ruth shook her head. "I didn't say that at all. When you parted with Callum, can you tell us which direction he set off in?"

Belinda growled. "The opposite direction to me," she snapped.

Not helpful. Maybe I'm guilty of getting her back up. Ruth smiled briefly and asked, "Which was?"

Belinda slammed a clenched fist onto the arm of the couch. "I don't know. I turned around and came back here. He went in the opposite direction, is that clear enough for you?"

"Thank you. That's much clearer." It wasn't, but Ruth wasn't about to let her know that, seeing how aggressive Belinda was becoming.

"How on earth you run a private investigation agency...well, it's beyond me. You should be out there, not stuck in here asking such stupid questions. My husband has been missing around fifteen hours at least and, for all we know, he could be injured and in need of our help. Or even worse than that." She broke down again.

Cynthia moved along the couch to comfort Belinda. "There, there, we mustn't think like that. Why don't we just tell Ruth what we know and let her begin her investigation?"

Belinda glared at Cynthia. "What do you think I've been doing for the past fifteen minutes? I'm getting the impression that you all think I have something to do with his disappearance."

Cynthia gasped and placed a hand over her chest as if she'd been struck in the heart with a knife. "Don't be so absurd. I'm offended by that remark, Belinda."

Ruth glanced at James and rolled her eyes. "Ladies, no one is suggesting anything of the sort. Belinda, all I'm doing is trying my hardest to ascertain your husband's final movements before he went missing. If you'd rather dispense with my services and leave the local police to deal with this, then fine. I'll bid you good day now and get on with enjoying my day off."

Belinda's fists clenched and unclenched a few times. "If you can't be bothered to take on the case, that's your prerogative. I'll find someone who can. Maybe we should leave it to the police to deal with rather than a second-rate private investigator."

Ruth had heard enough. She tucked her notebook in her bag and rose from her seat. "If that's how you feel, then so be it. I hope you find your husband soon." She turned towards the living room door.

"Ruth, please, don't listen to her, she's confused, doesn't know what she's saying. For the sake of our friendship, please, please, don't turn your back on us. We need you," Cynthia pleaded.

"I'm sorry. I didn't mean to verbally attack you. I'm worried about my husband and lashing out. Please forgive me?" Belinda asked, her voice trembling a little.

Turning to face the other occupants in the room, Ruth let out an exasperated breath and shrugged. "I'll try and find your husband but I won't tolerate you thinking I'm not up to the job. In the past four to five months I've solved two major cases in this town before the head of the local police even got on the starting blocks. My record speaks for itself. I know you're an outsider, but Cynthia's words of praise should be enough to put your mind at ease."

"I'm sorry for my foolish behaviour. In the circumstances, I'm hoping you will forgive me?" Belinda's head bowed in regret.

"Okay. We can start over if that's what you want. I will ask the simplest of questions in order to get to the truth. If you find them a struggle to answer, believing them to be futile, then I don't see a way around that."

Belinda let out a weighty sigh. "I've apologised, what more do you want me to do?"

"You can let me get on with my job, after you've given me all the facts."

"I have told you everything. I'm getting the impression that you don't believe me, though."

"I do believe you. Okay, let's move on. Was Callum worried about anything?"

"Such as?" Belinda tilted her head to ask.

"I don't know, was he in debt perhaps?"

"No, he's never been in debt in his life, as far as I know."

Ruth jotted down her answers in her notebook, her mind whirring with further questions as she wrote. "Is he ill?"

"No. He's as healthy as any other sixty-six-year-old man I know," Belinda replied, speaking to Ruth pleasantly for the first time.

"That's good to know, especially taking into consideration the weather we had last night. How long have you been married?"

"Ten years this year."

"Have either of you been married before?"

"Yes. We're both on speaking terms with our exes, if that's what you're going to ask next?"

"I was. Thank you. Where do you live?"

"About an hour from here, in Timbleton. Why?"

"I'm wondering if Callum could have become disorientated at all, possibly jumped in a taxi and returned home."

Belinda gasped. "We never thought of that, did we, Cynthia?" She picked up her handbag, lying on the floor next to her, and took out her mobile. "I'll ring home now."

They waited for the phone to connect. It proved pointless. It rang and rang until Belinda ended the call.

"Asking the most obvious question here: does your husband have a mobile?" Belinda nodded. "I suppose you've tried ringing that?"

"Yes, every hour. There's no answer. Now do you see why I'm so worried?"

"I do. Last question for now. Do you have a recent photo of Callum?"

Belinda flicked through the photos on her phone and handed it to Ruth. "This was taken a few days ago."

Ruth took a picture of the man on her own phone; she'd use that to question the locals. "Thank you, that will be a great help." She returned the phone to Belinda.

"Please, there truly is no reason for my husband to disappear like this. In my heart of hearts, I believe something dreadful has happened to him. Do you want us to help you in your search?"

"No. The weather is against us on this one. It would be better if you all stayed here and left that side of things to us. If he wants to be found, we'll find him."

"By that I take it you think he's hiding somewhere, is that it?" Reg asked.

Ruth shrugged. "The honest answer is, I don't know what to think yet. We'll get off and begin our search. We'll be in touch as soon as we find out anything, I promise. Try not to worry in the meantime."

"Easier said than done, Ruth," Cynthia replied, getting to her feet.

Ruth and James rose from their seats and walked towards the door.

"Good luck," Belinda called after them.

Outside the house, Ruth took the opportunity to speak to Cynthia alone. "What's your take on what's gone on?" she asked.

Cynthia shrugged. "I really couldn't tell you."

"You told me you thought he was henpecked when we met the other day. Do you stand by that statement?"

"I can't remember actually saying those words, but yes, I suppose you're right. I got the impression that Belinda dictated what Callum did, where and when. He didn't appear to have a life of his own. Oh gosh, that sounds so harsh. You don't think she's done anything to him, do you?"

"To be honest with you, I find her very hard to read at this time. Her emotions are swinging all over the place."

"Oh my, if she has done something to him, then I won't feel safe in my own home."

Ruth touched Cynthia's forearm. "Try not to consider the worst. I'm sure we'll find him once we begin our search. Try and remain calm. If he should show up, ring me straight away. We'll report back in a few hours whether we find him or not."

"We need to discuss your fee," Cynthia said. "No, we don't. I trust you not to rip us off."

Ruth smiled. "I'd never rip off a friend. I'll charge you a fair rate. The quicker we get going, the less money it'll cost you," she added.

"It was wrong of me to bring money into this. Please forgive me, Ruth?"

"Nonsense, there's nothing to forgive. Speak later."

"Good luck." Cynthia waved them off and remained at the door until Ruth and James got into her car, Betty.

Ruth started the engine and waved a final time at her friend who finally closed the door.

James let out a long breath. "Not sure how to read this one. What about you, love?"

Ruth drove away from the house and headed into town. "Me neither. She's an odd one. The wife, I mean, not Cynthia."

"She is. Why would her husband take off like that? We all have arguments, but I would never leave you alone in town."

"Let's face it, I wouldn't allow you to. It's perplexing. I hope we find him. Do you think it's likely that he might have had enough and tried to find his way back home, possibly hitched a lift with someone?"

"That would be a dangerous scenario right there. Who knows who's lurking on the streets nowadays?"

"Said like a true copper who doesn't tend to trust anyone."

James laughed. "I'd rather be like that than have someone pull the wool over my eyes and make a fool out of me."

He had a point. He'd never fallen out with someone because they'd ripped him off. "Where do we start?"

"The coffee shop seems as good a place as any."

Ruth drove down the high street and pulled up outside Maggie's coffee shop. They left the car's windows open for Ben and entered the shop. Maggie Denton, who was an old school friend of Ruth's, glanced up and smiled at them.

"Hello, stranger. What brings you in here?"

"Business. How are you, Maggie?" Ruth leaned over the counter and kissed her on the cheek. "You remember James, don't you?"

"I do. I hear congratulations are in order. When's the big day?"

Ruth shuffled her feet a little, trying to think of an adequate response in front of James, without it seeming as though she wasn't looking forward to their wedding. "We haven't decided yet."

"Well, it took you long enough to accept this handsome young man's proposal. Don't take forever setting the date, Ruth."

"I won't, or should I say, we won't."

James remained silent on the matter.

"Anyway, I'm working a case at the moment and wondered if you can help me."

"Me? How?" Maggie asked, frowning.

"One of my friends, Cynthia Jackson, has visitors staying with her the weekend. Well, yesterday the couple went for a walk, and the husband hasn't been seen since." She fished out her mobile and showed the photo of Callum to Maggie.

"Crikey! He was in here yesterday." Her voice lowered. "I remember thinking what a nice man he was. Very polite; however, he seemed fairly quiet during their drink. She did most of the talking. Very animated she was, too. Gesturing with her hands and folding her arms with a determined expression fixed on her face."

Is that so? "And he hardly said anything, is that right?"

"Yeah, the poor man gave me the impression that he was under the thumb. Dared not speak, not that she took a breath to let him get a word in." Maggie raised her hand. "I might be doing her an injustice there, so ignore me."

"But that's how it looked to you, an outsider, yes?"

Maggie folded her arms. "It did. He seemed a decent enough chap, good manners and inoffensive."

"And you didn't take to her at all?" Ruth enquired, trusting Maggie's instincts were on a par with her own.

"Like I said, she was offish towards him. I hate it when people display their anger outside of their own home. Why subject other people to that crap?"

"Exactly. Okay, how long did they stay?"

"Long enough to finish their drinks. They were my last customers for the day. I closed up shortly after they left around five to six."

"Excellent. Did you see which direction they went in?"

She pointed to the right. "That way."

"Did you see them again?"

"Actually, when I was leaving, around six-thirty, I saw her. He was nowhere to be seen. She was looking in one of the shop windows, the charity shop, up the road."

"And he wasn't around? Are you sure?"

"Definite. I pumped the air with my fist, thought good for him for doing the right thing and leaving her to listen to her own voice."

"He hasn't been seen since."

"Since last night? Oh heck."

"So it would appear, yes. We're going to check the town and then the coastline. Can you do me a favour and ask your customers if they've seen a stranger, appearing to be lost, around today?"

"I will, of course, I will. Oh my, who'd have thought it? I hope you find him. He wasn't ill, was he? You know, some form of dementia perhaps? You know my dad's got that, don't you? He's been declining rapidly over the past year. He doesn't even recognise me when I pay him a visit at the home now." Tears appeared in her brown eyes.

"Oh, Maggie, I hadn't heard. I'm so sorry. That must be hard on you and your family."

"My brother, Jed, has taken it badly. He breaks down every time he sees him. I've told him to stay away for both their sakes. Mum is lost. She keeps cooking meals for two, thinking Dad is coming home for his dinner. I'm concerned for her well-being. She visits Dad regularly but bursts into tears the second she leaves him. They've just celebrated their fortieth wedding anniversary. The home put on a small party for them, but Dad didn't have a clue what was going on. He sat staring at the TV the whole time she was there."

"How dreadful for you."

"The doctor has told us to expect the worst but also said that people in Father's state can last for years."

"Hey, if ever you want to chat, you know where to find me. A problem shared and all that."

"You have enough on your plate as it is. We'll survive. We have to in the end. Dementia is the pits. It destroys the people we love and causes them to become strangers, that's the hardest part."

Ruth went around the counter and hugged her friend.

Maggie sobbed and clung to her. Eventually, she stepped back and apologised. "I'm sorry, you didn't ask for that. I'm fine, honestly I am. I've come to terms with it now. Dad died the second the disease took hold of him. I know that's a terrible thing to say, but it's the truth. We're waiting for the day to come now."

"Try to remain positive. The scientists are doing their utmost to come up with a cure. I read it in an article only last week, sweetie."

"You haven't seen him, Ruth. He's gone too far to be saved now.

Maybe our generation will benefit from what they're coming up with as a cure, but not Dad, he's too far gone."

Ruth returned to the other side of the counter and wiped a stray tear from her cheek. She felt fortunate her parents were both in good health and out there, intent on enjoying what was left of their lives. "I meant what I said. If you need someone to share the burden, give me a call."

"You're too kind. Thanks. I hope you find this chappie and that he hasn't got the dreaded D-disease."

"His wife didn't mention he had it, so fingers crossed. Speak soon. Ring me if you need me, okay?"

"You're a good friend, Ruth."

She smiled, and together, she and James left the café. They continued along the row of shops, some of which were seasonal and had closed their doors for the winter months. Ruth showed each of the shop owners, or managers, the photo of Callum. Unfortunately, no one recognised him. Several hours into their mission, and at the last shop they tried, they were offered a lifeline.

Nancy Wilder, owner of the best patisserie within a thirty-mile radius, recalled seeing the couple. Ruth whipped out her notebook and jotted the details down as Nancy recalled them.

"I thought it strange, one minute the woman was pointing at the wedding display in the window, and the next the man went storming off. She shouted after him. Don't ask me what she said, I was distracted serving a customer at the time so I couldn't give the couple my full attention."

"That's okay. Did you happen to see which direction the man was heading in?"

"Well, she went up the high street, and he went towards the beach or the pier—it was in that direction anyway."

"Thanks, Nancy, that's a huge help."

"Hardly, I wish I could tell you more. The truth is, by the time my customers left it was a good fifteen minutes later. I did take a quick look up and down the road but couldn't see either of them. What happened? A lovers' tiff?"

"We're not sure right now. All we know is that Callum went missing around the time you last saw him."

She shook her head and muttered as if the walls had ears, "I hope that damned wife of his feels guilty. The way she was shouting at him was atrocious."

Ruth inclined her head. "In what way? Wasn't it just like an ordinary couple's argument? I thought you didn't hear what they were saying because you were dealing with your customers?"

"A deaf person would have been able to have read the anger pouring out of that woman. I didn't have to hear what was being said. Her sign language was enough to reveal what kind of mood she was in. I felt sorry for the man."

"Was it an argument or was it one-sided, her doing all the shouting?"

"Maybe that's what was making her so irate," Nancy suggested. "I know what I'm like with my old man once we start a barney. He knows he never wins so tends to clam up pretty darn quickly," she added with a smile.

Ruth turned to face James. He shook his head, and a silent warning not to get involved passed between them.

"I recognise that look. You two have years ahead of you to join the club of warring couples. You're both young, and there's no gold band on that finger of yours yet, Ruth. While we're on the subject of your upcoming wedding, don't forget I make award-winning wedding cakes. And yes, that was a huge hint from me. Always one to tout for business when the opportunity arises."

Ruth chuckled, admiring the woman's cheekiness. "You'll be one of the first people we contact once we start planning the wedding details, I promise you. Was there anything else about this couple that struck you as odd, Nancy?"

She paused and stared at the beautiful display of chocolate gâteaux off to her left as if seeking extra help. "No, I don't think so. What I've told you already should give you enough clues to know that the couple didn't get on. Let me rephrase that: they weren't getting on at the time. Whether they got on ordinarily, I wouldn't have a clue about that.

Would anyone?" She leaned forward and whispered, "Do any of us really have an inkling what goes on behind the closed doors of other people's homes."

"True enough, I suppose. Okay, we'll be off. We want to continue the search before the weather gets any worse. They forecast a large storm coming in from France this evening. If you should see this man, do me a favour, ask him in for a drink and ring me right away."

"Of course. I'll tie him down if necessary until you arrive."

"I admire your enthusiasm; the call will suffice. I can be here within a few minutes."

"I'll do that. I hope you find the chap. He had a kind face, unlike that wife of his. Gosh, there I go again, presuming they're married."

Ruth sniggered. "Your instincts are right, they are married. Is it any wonder I've dug my heels in about walking down the aisle over the years?"

James stood on her foot. She issued an embarrassed smile and bid Nancy farewell. Ruth cringed, aware James was probably about to have a go at her the second they stepped outside the shop. She kissed him. "Don't judge me for what comes out of my mouth."

"You're unbelievable at times. It's a good job I love you. Where next?"

"I think we need to take a break. Ben has only had a few trots up and down the high street in between our visits. He's usually had at least ten runs by now on a normal working day."

James stared at her, gaping.

"What? I'm self-employed. He's part of the package and needs time off from lying in his bed all day. Give me a break."

He shook his head and hooked his arm through hers. Together, they battled their way back to the car through the bracing wind ripping down the high street.

"This weather is getting worse by the hour. I hope we find Callum soon. I fear for his safety if we don't," James stated while Ruth unhitched Ben from the safety harness in the back seat. He licked her face as if greeting a long-lost companion.

"Did you miss me, boy?"

Ben moaned and licked her cheek again.

James tutted behind her and suggested, "Okay, why don't we head down to the beach? We can let Ben have a run and search for Callum at the same time." He slung an arm around her shoulder. The three of them braced themselves against the wind and the drizzle that had begun to fall.

"Great, just what we need to hamper us," she complained, zipping up her coat and flipping on her hood.

"At least you've got a hood to your jacket. I foresee me being a drowned rat before long."

"You'll be my drowned rat." She grinned and pecked him on the cheek.

Once they were on the edge of the beach, Ruth removed Ben's leash. He bounded ahead of them. It didn't come as a surprise to find they were the only ones who'd ventured down there. Mind you, time was getting on, and she imagined the majority of Carmel Cove's residents tucking in to a warming Sunday roast by now. Her stomach grumbled at the thought.

"We should get some food soon," James said.

"Give it half an hour or so. It shouldn't take us too long to search the beach and the cove."

"If you say so. It's a pretty large area if we're going to do a thorough search. What if this proves to be a waste of time, what then?"

"Ever the pessimist. I'm not sure. I suppose we should head up the hill and check the coastal path. He might have gone up there."

"You think? In this bad weather, and on foot? I can't see the logic in that."

She shrugged. "If you have a better idea, feel free to share it. The man was obviously troubled about something if what the two witnesses have told us is true."

"Maybe we should turn back and question his wife properly in that case."

"Perhaps. Let's not give up just yet. Anyway, Ben needs a good run after being cooped up in the car for so long. He's just not used to it."

James grumbled something that she didn't quite catch, but Ruth wasn't in the mood to ask him to repeat it, fearing it could lead to another argument between them.

"How do you want to do this? You search at the back of the beach near the rocks and I check near the sea, or what?" she asked, peering out at the waves that were already increasing in size due to the bracing wind.

"Sounds good to me. Don't go too close to the edge, those waves look bad."

She saluted him with her right hand. "Yes, boss."

They parted, and as Ruth checked the coastline, she threw large pebbles for Ben to fetch, although as there were so many, once he set off after one, he soon got confused and stared back at her as if to say, "Are you having a laugh or what?" She laughed at her companion several times during their stroll.

There were days when she loved a walk by the sea when it was rough. It cleared the cobwebs from her mind. After ten minutes or so, Ruth and Ben reached the rugged coastline of the cove, where the headland jutted out into the sea. She cautiously approached the area, keeping hold of Ben's collar as she tried to peer around the large boulder-type rocks. As far as she could tell, there was nothing there. James joined her a few moments later and shook his head.

"Nothing?" she asked, pondering what to do next.

"Nope."

"What about going around the headland, would that be possible?"

James hitched up his right shoulder. "Possibly, if the tide was out. I haven't really been down here for years. I used to explore this coastline as a child, but the erosion has altered the headland considerably since then."

"That's a consideration I hadn't thought about. I'm unsure about the tides around here. We rarely come down here."

"You should reconsider that notion. Ben seems to love it at the beach."

Ben looked up and barked when he heard his name, and they both laughed.

"And you reckon he doesn't understand."

"Okay, I was wrong about that. Shall we head back to the car now? I'm perished, and it's getting colder."

James' words were like a dagger to her chest. She shook her head. "Poor Callum. If he's still exposed to these conditions, he's not likely to last long, is he?"

"Sadly, I have to agree with you. Mind you, it was daft of him taking off like that in the first place."

"Maybe that was his intention."

"What, to go missing on purpose, is that what you're saying?"

"Why not? I read a scary statistic last week that over eighteen thousand people went missing last year alone."

"And how many of those showed up a few days or weeks later?"

"Not sure on the timeline, but of those eighteen thousand, over eighteen hundred people remained on the missing register after a year. Maybe they'd had enough of their surroundings and just felt the need to start afresh somewhere new."

"Let's face it, Belinda doesn't seem to be a barrel of laughs to live with, does she?"

"I think that's a tad unfair. The poor woman is distraught, out of her mind with worry."

"Hmm…it didn't come across that way to me. You're forgetting what the witnesses have told us, too."

James kicked out at a pebble and then picked up a flat one which he threw out to sea. Ben took off after it before either of them could stop him. Fortunately, the dog had more sense than to dive into the fierce waves heading his way.

Ruth slapped James on the arm. "Think about what you're doing when Ben's around."

"Sorry, I forgot for a moment. He stopped, though."

"That's because he has far more sense than you." She sniggered.

"I'll ignore that. We should get on. Swap places? You take the high road this time?"

"Agreed. Then I think we should head home for some much-needed grub. I know a tin of tomato soup has my name on it."

"Don't. That sounds wonderful, just what the doctor ordered on a blustery day like today. Let's get this over with. Hey, I've just had a thought… We don't venture out much, not into town anyway, on a Sunday. I'm shocked at how many shops are open, aren't you?"

"It's the winter, everyone is finding it tough, I guess. The trading laws are in place though, so they're probably only open ten to four. Look at me, I'm self-employed and working on a Sunday. Needs must."

"I'm not. I'm salaried. Can I remind you that I'm freezing my bits off just to help you out?"

She grinned. "And because you love me, of course. I appreciate all you do for me, James. If you want to call it a day and go home early, don't let me stop you."

"God, did I say that? A promise is a promise, and I would never let you be out on your own in this foul weather. Let's get on with it."

Ruth smiled and called Ben to heel, then she headed across the stones and patches of wet sand to the rocky area at the rear of the beach. Her heart was heavy. If James hadn't managed to find anything amongst the rocks, then the likelihood of her discovering anything was probably zero percent.

Ben helped in the search as best he could. He ran over the large stones the council had winched into position as a defence against the damaging waves the year before. She watched him keep his balance where she'd have likely slipped and hurt her ankle. She laughed at Ben as he tugged on a large piece of seaweed that a gull had obviously dropped on the rocks as it was the only piece in the vicinity, as opposed to the type she and Ben had walked through lower down the beach.

Her thoughts turned to satisfying her stomach and whether they had any fresh bread out to make toast to accompany her bowl of soup. It was Ben's insistent barking that broke into her reverie. "What is it, Ben, what have you found?" She stepped closer to the rocks, thinking that perhaps Ben had stumbled across a nest of sorts.

She peered over at James to see if he'd heard the commotion—he hadn't, he was still scouring the edge of the beach.

"James, James, over here." She waved her arms frantically but failed to gain his attention. "I'll be right back, boy. Stay there. Don't move." She tried to pick out a recognisable spot in case Ben followed her. There was a boulder with a trail of seagull droppings close to where Ben was standing. His barking had become more intense, and his voice was sounding strained now. She twisted back in James' direction. He was oblivious to what was going on.

With no other option left open to her, Ruth high-tailed it back towards the waves. She was breathless by the time she caught up to James. She bent over, her hands on her knees, panting fast and furious. "Didn't you hear me?"

"Obviously," James retorted sarcastically.

Ben joined them and sat beside Ruth. She gulped down some fresh air and pointed back up the beach. "Ben. I think he's found something behind the rocks... I need you to come and check for me in case it's a bird or something. You know how scared I am of them... You need to investigate it for me." She didn't give him a chance to answer, just wrenched his arm and set off.

Ben ran ahead of them. Halfway between the rocks and where Ruth and James were, he turned back to check if they were still following him. She found the marker rock and urged James to take a closer look.

"There. Ben will show you the exact position, go with him." She gave him an encouraging push in the back.

"Will you stop that? I could slip on the rocks if I'm not careful."

"Is that why you didn't check them thoroughly before?"

"Give it a rest, Ruth. Let's see what Ben's found first, then make the judgement whether I did the right thing or not, okay?"

"Get on with it, James, please?"

He leaned forward to grip the boulder with his gloved hands then followed Ben up the rock face. Ben started barking again.

"There. He's showing you where he wants to take you. Good boy, Ben."

James tutted as his shoes refused to take hold in any of the crevices he could find. "This is going to be impossible to climb from this angle. I need to work my way back, choose an easier route on the rocks lower down. It's treacherous because of the rain. I don't fancy breaking my neck in the process, just to see what is driving Ben nuts."

Ruth sighed. "Okay, I hear you. Hurry, though, James, this is totally out of character for Ben."

"It might be; however, you said yourself that he's not been down here before, so it's probably something strange he's located. Might even be a seal pup for all we know. Give me a chance to get in there and take a look."

"Okay, hurry up, please," she replied, sensing something was amiss.

He located a smaller boulder and managed to climb to the top without injuring himself. He stood upright and slipped back down to the beach, cussing as he hit and sank into the wet sand below.

"Don't stand up next time. Crawl on your hands and knees if you have to."

He shook his head and concentrated on climbing the rock again. This time he balanced on all fours and scrambled across the top of the rocks. He leapt onto the larger rock and peered into the crevice where Ben's nose was pointing. He groaned and looked down at Ruth. "You'd better ring the boys in blue. I've just found Callum...he's dead."

4

*R*uth placed the call and then passed James her phone. "Compare him to the photo."

He shook his head, refusing to touch the mobile. "I don't have to, Ruth. I've seen the photo enough to know it's him."

"Bugger, I can't ring his wife. I need to tell her in person. Now I'm torn."

James slid down from the huge boulder and tilted his head. "Torn? About what?"

"I need to report back, and soon, but I'm tempted to remain here to see what the police have to say."

James cleared his throat. "Ahem, I'm the police or are you forgetting that?"

She tutted. "You know what I'm getting at. You don't count." She cringed, realising her mistake, and then rubbed his arm. "I'm sorry, that came out wrong. I didn't mean that."

"You really need to start paying attention to what comes out of your mouth. At times it can be highly offensive." He glared at her, and she shrivelled into her coat.

"Sorry. Forgive me?"

"Not for a few hours. Maybe you should wait for me in the car?"

"No way. This is my case, and I'm staying right here. Don't you go getting all high and mighty with me."

"I wasn't, I was merely stating facts." He turned his back and stomped his feet against the cold chill that seemed to be far worse now that they'd discovered Callum Carter's body.

She was aware she had some making up to do with her fiancé later; for now, though, she was too busy hoping her archenemy didn't show up and take over the case.

Within ten minutes, the beach was swarming with uniformed police, and striding towards them was the one person Ruth hated most in this world, DI Janice Littlejohn. Behind her was her equally abhorrent sidekick, DS Joe Kenton.

Littlejohn disregarded Ruth when she came to a stop in front of them. Instead, she spoke to James. "What's she doing here? Who found the body?"

Ruth stood tall, her shoulders pulled back. "Actually, that was me. Or more to the point, my dog. I called the police, like the good PI I am."

Littlejohn's sour gaze turned her way. "You, do something right for a change? That'll be the day." She tilted her head back and let out a derisory laugh.

Seething, Ruth swallowed down the mounting anger and glared at her. "In my job, I'll have you know I do lots of things right. It's how you perceive them where the problem lies, Inspector. That says more about you than it does about me." Again, as soon as the words hit the air, she regretted saying them. Out of the corner of her eye, James faced her and she could have sworn she heard him tut a little. *Tough, I'm not about to be browbeaten by the likes of her.*

"If I might say something, ma'am?" James asked, seeking Littlejohn's permission to speak.

She nodded curtly.

"This is Ruth's case. She has been employed by the deceased's wife to try and find him."

"Find him?" Littlejohn interrupted. "Was he missing?"

"Yes," Ruth replied, jumping in ahead of James. "He was a missing person, only your lot weren't interested when his wife tried to report his disappearance, and now the poor man is dead."

"*Our lot* as you so politely put it, Miss Morgan, have procedures in place that need to be followed. How long had the deceased been missing?"

Ruth knew when she was beaten. She lowered her voice and muttered, "Around six last night."

"Ah-hah! Less than twenty-four hours, which is the minimum time the law allows. Correct me if I'm wrong about that."

"You're not," Ruth agreed reluctantly.

"Okay, now we're here, I'm going to ask you both to step behind the cordon my lads are about to erect. You know the rules as well as I do, civilians aren't allowed near a scene."

"That's a crime scene? We don't know that's the case yet," Ruth chipped in.

"A man sets out on a walk and dies on the rocks on a deserted beach, and you wouldn't class it as a crime scene? What type of PI are you, Miss Morgan?" Littlejohn demanded, apparently seizing the opportunity to strike a blow to Ruth's gut.

"A successful one who has managed to solve her last two murder cases before the local police had even had their first coffee of the day."

James groaned beside her and kicked at a pebble close to his foot.

"I've heard enough. We're wasting time here, now. I've told you what I expect from you, now, move it. You, too, constable. Better still, why don't you take your interfering fiancée home with you?"

"Yes, boss. I'll do that now." He grasped Ruth's arm, urging her to leave the beach.

Ruth wrenched her arm away. "I haven't finished yet. My client has a right to know the cause of death."

"Your client will be informed, by me, at the appropriate time. Kenton, get the deceased's next of kin details down, would you?"

"Yes, boss." Kenton fished his notebook out of his pocket and held his pen in place, poised and ready for action.

Ruth threw her hand in the air and stormed off, leaving James to fill in the blanks for Littlejohn and her gormless crony.

James joined Ruth back at the car five minutes later. She was still seething.

"When are you going to learn not to swap insults with her, Ruth? This town isn't large enough for you and her to avoid each other. Why don't you accept that and move on? She has the law on her side, *you* don't."

"Do you want to walk home?" she snapped at him.

"Now you're just being childish."

"You told me she'd softened and would be more accepting of me in the future. Maybe that particular memo got lost on her desk."

"Seriously, Ruth, you need to wind in that neck of yours. You didn't even give her a chance when she arrived at the scene. Have you any idea how that's going to look for me at work? You know she takes out her bad mood on me. The bad moods you damn well put her in, I hasten to add."

"So leave. What's stopping you?"

He ran his hands through his hair, pulled it at the roots and let out a sigh full of steam. "I give up. We keep going over the same ground, time and time again. I've had enough of it, you hear me? It's too much, I can't take the hassle any more."

Perplexed, she demanded, "What's that supposed to mean?"

"I'm packing a bag when I get home. I'll go and stay with Frank for a few days. At the moment, I don't want to be anywhere near you."

She reached across him and threw open the car door. "You'll be better off walking home in that case."

"I guess I will." He slammed the door on the way out.

Ben whimpered in the back seat. She stroked him, trying her best to reassure him everything would be okay, even though huge doubts rattled her mind. James was running out on her, at the time she needed him the most. She couldn't think about that now, harsh but true. She owed it to her client to let her know that Callum's body had been found.

Ruth arrived at the Old Station House to find Cynthia peering out of the lounge window. Ruth patted Ben on the head, wound down the back windows a little and left the car. She gulped in a lungful of bracing fresh air in readiness for what she was about to do. It felt odd not having James by her side, but somehow, she managed to push the sense of abandonment aside as she walked up the front path to the door.

Cynthia greeted her with a hug. "Hello, love, you look perished. Any news?"

Ruth nodded. "Yes, it's not the news we were hoping for, I'm sorry."

A scream echoed through the house. Not from Cynthia. Belinda had appeared in the doorway to the lounge and had put two and two together. *Great! Could this damn day get any worse?*

Cynthia dashed to Belinda's aid, catching the woman as her legs gave way beneath her. Ruth rushed to help them both. "I'm so sorry, Belinda. I never meant for you to hear like that. Let's get you back in the lounge."

Cynthia's husband, Reg, was on his feet, standing at the drinks' cabinet in the corner of the room, pouring brandy into a tumbler. Ruth and Cynthia stood on either side of Belinda and eased her onto the couch. Reg swiftly appeared beside Ruth and handed Belinda the brandy.

"Drink this, love, it'll help with the shock." He returned to the cabinet and asked, "Anyone else want one?"

Cynthia nodded.

"Not for me, I'm driving," Ruth replied, resisting the temptation to drown her own sorrows in a glass.

"Where's James?" Cynthia asked, breaking the silence.

"He had stuff to do at home." *Like pack his bags.*

"What happened?" Belinda asked through the sobs.

Cynthia handed her the box of tissues. Belinda plucked a couple and blew her nose.

"We searched everywhere for him. Finally, we took Ben with us to the beach, and he discovered Callum on the rocks."

"How did he get there?" Cynthia asked. "If it's the ones I think you mean, they're huge, aren't they?"

"Your guess is as good as mine. Even James had trouble getting up them."

"He loved rock climbing back in the day," Reg offered. "Always the first to tackle an unclimbable terrain when we were serving."

"Ah, that explains it then. Maybe he lost his footing and hit his head. We won't know the actual cause of death until the post-mortem has been performed. I'm so sorry I wasn't able to find him sooner, Belinda."

"Do you know when it happened?" she asked tearfully.

"No. We questioned a few of the local residents in the shops in town, and they told us they saw him heading towards the beach. My guess is he probably wandered down there for a while, maybe he tried to get up on the rocks for a better view of the sea, and that's when the accident occurred."

"You definitely think it was an accident then?" Cynthia asked, her hands twisting a tissue in her lap.

"Like I said, we won't know until the PM results are confirmed."

"When is that likely to be?" Belinda asked, sniffling. "I need to get back home and sort out the arrangements for his funeral. Never thought I'd be doing that at his time of life. He was a fit man, we both thought he had years ahead of him. Now, he's gone…oh God, I don't think I'm going to cope without him in my life. He was my soul mate. All right, we might have fallen out now and again, every couple does that, don't they?" She searched the other people in the room, hoping for some form of agreement to her statement.

Ruth was tempted to raise her hand to concur, having fallen out with James barely ten minutes earlier.

"It's inevitable when folks reach retirement age and are around each other twenty-four- seven," Cynthia stated. "I'm so sorry. If you hadn't come to visit us, this wouldn't have happened."

"That's nonsense, Cyn, we're not to blame for this," Reg reprimanded her gently.

Cynthia shook her head, and tears rolled down her cheeks. "No matter what anyone says, the truth remains the same. Callum was climbing the rocks on our local beach when his life was ended. If he hadn't come here, he'd still be alive today."

A car door slammed and Ruth rushed to the window. She gulped and groaned inwardly. Littlejohn was standing at the gate, glaring at her, her eyes narrowing in anger as she approached the house.

Ruth rushed into the hallway and opened the front door. "Can you leave your venomous tongue at the threshold?"

"I beg your pardon? How dare you speak to me like that, Morgan? What are you doing here? I told you to leave this investigation to me."

"I had every right telling my client what I had discovered. She's the one paying my wages, not you."

Littlejohn chewed on the inside of her mouth. Ruth could tell her anger was building and she was about to explode.

"Kenton, get her out of my way."

The sergeant passed Littlejohn and yanked on Ruth's arm.

"Get off her. I don't have the slightest idea who you are, but Ruth is a guest in my home, unlike you. Stop manhandling her this instant." Cynthia shouted, clearly livid.

Littlejohn had the grace to look embarrassed by Cynthia's severe words. "I'm sorry. Miss Morgan and I are old foes. I'm DI Janice Littlejohn, the senior investigating officer on this case, and Miss Morgan is getting in the way of my investigation."

"What absolute poppycock. I told you to get your hands off her, young man. Either you do that or I'll get on the phone to your superior. Ruth has done nothing wrong. I've heard all there is to know about *you*, on the other hand. The less said about that the better, I think. Now, for the last time, let go of her." Cynthia exuded all the power of a British bulldog in her voice and in her actions as she personally ripped Kenton's hand from Ruth's arm.

"I apologise. We appear to have got off on the wrong foot," Littlejohn said sheepishly.

"*You* might have, not me. Say what you have to say and get out of my house."

"Now, Cynthia, give the woman a chance," Reg said behind them. "Won't you please come in, Inspector? Belinda is in the lounge. She's desperate to hear what you've learned about my good friend's death. Ladies, let the inspector and her sergeant pass."

Ruth and Cynthia took a step back, and Littlejohn passed them, displaying a triumphant smile that quickly slipped the second she entered the lounge.

"I'm sorry for your loss. I believe you're aware of your husband's death," Littlejohn announced in her usual offhand manner.

Ruth cringed at the woman's coldness towards Belinda and felt sorry for the woman, mourning her husband.

"Ruth told me where he was found, nothing else. What happened?" Belinda asked, her eyes wide with expectation.

Littlejohn shrugged. "We're not certain of the facts as yet. I wanted to come and offer my condolences and to assure you that we'll be doing all we can to try to ascertain how your husband died. We won't know much until the post-mortem results have been sent to me."

"Yes, Ruth told us that much," Cynthia butted in, hooking her arm through Ruth's and smiling at her.

Ruth patted Cynthia on the hand, her friendship meaning the world to her in the face of adversity.

"Miss Morgan was correct in her knowledge of police procedures in this instance. I know you employed her to track down your husband, which we're grateful for, but now, from this point forward, you'll be dealing with me, the senior investigating officer," Littlejohn repeated, in case anyone was uncertain of her position.

"We got that, Inspector," Cynthia blasted, clutching Ruth's arm tighter. "I trust Ruth implicitly, and if there were any suspicious circumstances to Callum's death, then I'd rather have Ruth still on the payroll to investigate what happened. Her record is exemplary, as you're aware."

Littlejohn's chest expanded. She let out the breath and forced a smile. "I don't think that's very wise. Miss Morgan has been guilty of getting in the way on some recent cases. I'd rather not let that happen this time."

Ruth went to open her mouth, but Cynthia squeezed her arm and said, "She's solved two major crimes in the time I've been a resident in this town. That alone shows how remarkable her detective skills are. Therefore, I stand by my decision to keep her employed to find out the cause of Callum's death. I believe we're all in agreement with that, too, yes, Reg and Belinda?"

Belinda appeared dumbstruck for a second or two. She nodded, and so did Reg.

"Very well. I would be willing to work with Miss Morgan on this case. We can set any differences we have aside for the time being, and she can share her findings with me the moment she uncovers any clues likely to lead to solving the case."

Before Ruth could say anything, Cynthia demanded, "Will you be doing the same with her? Sharing information?"

"No. It doesn't work like that. The police don't share information in a case with outsiders. Why should we?" Littlejohn's eyes widened at the thought.

"All is fair in love and war, Inspector. Then, I don't think Ruth should be forced to share any information with you either. She's a professional, after all, a damned good one. She must be to have beaten you to solving the last two cases, wouldn't you agree?"

On one hand, Ruth wished the ground would open up and swallow her, and on the other she was enjoying the way Cynthia was causing Littlejohn to squirm. It was as if she was secretly channelling her thoughts to Cynthia and she was firing them at Littlejohn with both barrels.

"I have better things to do than to continue this debate. Mrs Carter, is there somewhere we can speak privately?"

Belinda glanced up at Reg who was standing beside her. He placed a hand on her shoulder. "She's fine where she is, with us surrounding her for support. Ask your questions, Inspector."

Littlejohn shot Ruth a glance which she found impossible to read. *Is she seeking my help with the situation? Or warning me to leave?* She shrugged. It was obvious Cynthia and the rest of them preferred it if she remained exactly where she was. She propped herself up against the oak sideboard and folded her arms. Littlejohn seemed livid, judging by the amount of steam coming out of her ears. *Tough, lady!*

The inspector turned her attention to Belinda and asked, "If it's not too much trouble, perhaps you can tell me what happened prior to your husband's disappearance."

Belinda looked over at Ruth for guidance. "I've already been through this with Ruth. I'm giving her my permission to answer that for me."

"With respect, Mrs Carter, it's your opinion I'm seeking, no one else's, at this stage."

"I'm too distraught. Why should I be forced to go over things when Ruth knows exactly what went on?"

"It's called cooperating with the police and their enquiries. As I've already stated, Miss Morgan has nothing to do with either this investigation or the police."

"Well, I'm tired and grieving." Belinda swivelled in her seat to face Cynthia. "What should I do, Cynthia?"

"We've already told the inspector that we're happy for Ruth to speak on your behalf. If she's not willing to accept that, then maybe we should ask her and her partner to leave."

Littlejohn cleared her throat. "That, in my opinion, would be a mistake from the outset, ladies. I've already given you my reasons for not involving Miss Morgan in the case. If it's too soon to speak to you then so be it. We'll leave now and request that you come down to the station to answer our questions if you won't speak to us here."

"What? You can do that?" Cynthia demanded. "Just like that? You're prepared to ride roughshod over a grieving widow's feelings? Without any consideration to her grief or the heartache she must be experiencing at this sad time?"

Littlejohn stared at Cynthia, eyes narrowed with hatred—at least that was how it appeared to Ruth. She decided to intervene before things became too heated.

"What harm can it do, Inspector? Please reconsider? Belinda is clearly upset by the loss of her husband. If you've ever lost a close member of your family, you'll know what she's going through right now."

"Thanks for the insight. And for your information, I have lost a close member of my family, only last year, in fact. My father died in a car accident. I worked with the police at the time to establish my father's movements prior to his death. Forgive me, but that's all I'm trying to do here."

The room fell silent for a few moments as the news sank in. A pang of pride rippled through Ruth's stomach. Maybe she was guilty of always thinking badly of the inspector when, at the end of the day, she was an officious nut, only trying her best to carry out her job.

"I'm sorry to hear that. A little compassion for Belinda shouldn't be a problem at all then," Ruth replied.

Littlejohn heaved out a resigned sigh, defeated in her exploits by the look of things. "Very well. I'll allow your intervention for now, Miss Morgan. We're wasting time. Please tell me what you know of the deceased's movements?"

Ruth recapped what Belinda had told her at the start of her investigation. "Hence the reason James and I were out on the beach today, searching for Callum."

"I see. May I ask what the argument was about, Mrs Carter?" Littlejohn asked.

Belinda frowned and shook her head slowly. "You know what? I can't remember off the top of my head. What do couples generally argue about? Trivial matters mostly."

"That might be the case ordinarily; however, forgive me for asking you to try to remember, as whatever it was about has likely contributed to your husband's death."

"Wow! Did you just say that?" Ruth butted in.

Littlejohn slowly turned to glare at her. "You have a problem with my choice of wording, Miss Morgan?"

"I do. I think your phraseology could be more tactful in the circumstances, Inspector."

Littlejohn's clenched fist hit her thigh. It was a small movement that Ruth easily detected. "A word in your ear, Miss Morgan, in private, if I may?"

"We won't be long," Ruth announced, following the fuming inspector out into the hallway.

She spun around to face Ruth and jabbed a finger repeatedly in her chest as she spoke. "I've had as much as I'm going to take from you. Your interference in this case is starting to get up my nose now, Miss Morgan."

"I assure you, it's not intentional. Look, why don't we agree to call a truce on this one? It's a perplexing case. At present we're at a loss to know how he died, whether there was any intent, or if he died of natural causes in the elements."

"I don't see how we can ever consider working together. You appear to have a massive chip on your shoulder which is proving to be hard to shift."

Ruth's eyes bulged. "What? I'm really not sure where you get that idea from. For your information, I do not have a chip on my shoulder. Cynthia has employed me to try to ascertain what happened to her friend. After all, I was the one who stumbled across his body in the search. Your lot refused to help. Yes, I know the rules, you're not at liberty to get involved until twenty-four hours have passed. Maybe if you had, Callum Carter might still be alive instead of lying dead on the beach."

"If you've quite finished slagging the police off in this area, Miss Morgan. I'm aware of what's gone on between us in the past. I'm also aware of your capabilities as a private investigator. I don't agree with them, as most of the time our paths cross because you tend to step on my toes. That's what grieves me about your input in a case. I think any other inspector would feel aggrieved in my position."

"That's something you're going to need to get your head around then, because believe me, Inspector, I'm not going anywhere until I find out how Callum Carter died. Whether he had a futile argument with his spouse before his death or not. It's obvious he died long after that occurred. His wife returned to the cottage around sevenish or thereabouts. We don't have a time of death for the victim yet, do we?"

"You know as well as I do, we won't obtain that information until the PM has been conducted."

"I know that, I'm not a novice. Sorry, I shouldn't have snapped. Maybe we're both guilty of rubbing each other up the wrong way."

"Seems that way to me. I can't promise to work with you on this one, Miss Morgan. For a start, I don't think my DCI would be too enthusiastic about that notion. However, I'm willing to draw a line under what's gone on in the past and move forward, if you are?"

"Is that because the family are objecting to your involvement in the case?" Ruth sniggered.

Littlejohn's expression was one of thunder, and Ruth instantly regretted her question. "Not in the slightest. Perhaps we're never going to get along enough to solve a case together."

"I'm sorry. My mouth has a tendency to run away from me at the most inopportune moment."

"I would never have guessed. If you can rein in that sarcastic streak of yours then maybe we can consider working alongside each other, if only to share details of the investigation."

"Two-sided?" Ruth asked, grinning.

"Yes. I'm putting my head on the block for you and your friends here, I hope you appreciate that. If my DCI gets wind of what I've just agreed to, I could be out on my ear and looking for another job. Maybe even banging on your door for work."

Ruth chuckled. "James is first in line for that role." *Or he was! Until he decided to throw in the towel and dump me. So much for having the security of wearing an engagement ring. A lot of good that's done either of us. Oh well, them's the breaks.*

"Talking of your fiancé, where is he?"

"I told him to go home. He'll be there now, preparing the Sunday roast, I shouldn't wonder," she replied, telling a white lie.

"You have a good man there. He obviously worships you. You're a very lucky lady, Miss Morgan."

"Thank you. It took me long enough to realise that." *And now I've blown it and he's at home packing a bag.* Sadness filled her heart. It would likely be hours before she left here, and that would be too late to try to convince him to stay.

"He's a good officer and has a bright future ahead of him. He's slipped up in the past, mainly due to leaking information to outsiders, namely *you*. There's no way a lower grade officer should be doing that. He had to be punished, I hope you agree?"

"That was my fault entirely. I put him in an invidious position. We've agreed he should take a back seat on any further cases that come my way." *Another white lie!*

Littlejohn cocked her head. "Really? I could have sworn I spoke to him at the crime scene...possibly my imagination playing tricks on me."

"He was there. I can't deny that. He's agreed not to get involved now, though."

Littlejohn snorted. "I wonder how long that is likely to last."

A cough from the lounge doorway interrupted them. It was Cynthia. "Sounds like you two are getting along at last. Belinda is keen to get on with things. She has family to consider and would like to start ringing them soon, you know, to share the awful news."

"We've agreed to work together on this case. I'll get all the details from Miss Morgan. Tell Mrs Carter she's free to inform her family."

Cynthia smiled broadly. "I had an inkling you two would come to your senses sooner or later. I'll tell her. Feel free to use the kitchen if you want to discuss the case in private. Just keep your hands off the cheesecake I made today to keep my anxiety in check."

"Will do, Cynthia. All right if we help ourselves to coffee?" Ruth asked, giving Cynthia a cheeky wink.

"Go on then, if you must. Although you know too much caffeine isn't good for you, don't you?"

Ruth led the way into the kitchen and shouted over her shoulder, "Whoever made up that fallacy obviously hasn't worked in the crime-solving industry."

"Hear, hear," Littlejohn agreed behind her.

Ruth chalked it up: Littlejohn agreeing with her. She filled the kettle and asked, "Coffee with milk and sugar?"

"Just milk for me. Trying to cut down on the excess calories."

Ruth ran her gaze over the length and breadth of the detective, at her odd lumpy bits here and there. "I know that feeling. Must be the amount of time we sit behind our desks that's the cause of piling on the pounds."

"There's nothing of you."

"I walk Ben at least four times a day. I suppose that keeps me fit in between jobs."

"How is the private investigator business in general?"

Pouring the boiled water into the cups, Ruth stirred the coffee and took it over to the table. They both sat and continued their conversation. "Hit and miss. It's going to be nice sinking my teeth into this investigation. What's your take on it? Did you see the body? I didn't get to see it," she added, looking over her shoulder at the door and lowering her voice.

"My partner saw it. His take is that it appeared the man hit the back of his head on the rocks. There was blood beneath his head, and his nose had also been bleeding."

"Interesting. Why am I not surprised to hear that? That terrain was terrible to climb. With the weather verging on storm-like conditions, I'm not surprised he took a tumble on the slippery rocks. Maybe he fell forwards and bashed his nose and then slipped backwards and hit his head on a jagged part of the boulder."

"Possibly. It's all supposition for now until the pathologist gives us his insight into what occurred." Littlejohn turned to glance at the doorway herself and then leaned forward to ask, "What's your take on the wife? Could this be a likely insurance payout scam?"

"I had my suspicions about her to begin with. Cynthia isn't too impressed with her visiting them. Callum was in the army with Reg, so the connection is with the men instead of the women. The witnesses I spoke to saw the couple argue and go their separate ways. Also, according to Reg, Callum was a keen mountain climber back in his army days. Perhaps he's guilty of momentarily forgetting his age, only to have regretted his actions when he fell."

"Plausible. Have you questioned the widow more thoroughly yet?"

"No, I've barely brushed the surface with my initial questions. It's the not knowing the circumstances behind his death, whether he fell or if he was pushed. We're going to be super reliant on the PM on this one. I'm inclined to let things lie as they are for now, although I appreciate how much that could jeopardise the case if the results come back that foul play was to blame for his death. It's a tough one as things stand."

"I think we need to ask her just in case. The results could take a few days to come back. If he was murdered, then his killer could still be around."

"I hear you. I agree, we should ask if everything was okay. Maybe it would be better to ask Cynthia those questions for now."

"Does she know the woman well enough to answer our questions, though?"

Ruth shrugged. "I could call her in and see what she knows."

"Do that. You've built up a rapport with the woman since she's arrived."

Ruth took a sip of her hot drink and then stood. "I'll ask her to join us."

She left the room and entered the lounge where she found Belinda on the phone, sobbing her heart out. She cringed at the woman's clear discomfort; however, it was nothing compared to what DS Kenton was feeling, judging by his appearance. He was standing in the bay window, his arms folded. He glanced over at Ruth and gave a brief nod.

"Cynthia," she whispered. "Could we have a quick word with you?"

Cynthia patted Belinda on the knee and left her seat. "With me? Where? In the kitchen?"

"Yes, it's nothing to worry about, I assure you."

The two women joined Inspector Littlejohn once more.

"Take a seat, Cynthia," Ruth instructed.

"Okay. What is it you need to know, ladies?"

Littlejohn smiled the briefest of smiles to put the woman at ease. "How well do you know the couple? The Carters?"

"Not very well really. Callum was with my husband in the army for around thirty years. Belinda came as part of the package when they've visited us in the past. They've been married ten years or so."

"Were they happy?" Littlejohn asked, jotting down the odd note in her little black book.

"They appeared to be. Well...let's see, I suppose you'd say it appeared they tolerated each other. Gosh, I hate saying that at a time like this."

"If it's the truth, then that's what I'm prepared to go with. Do you know what this argument was about?" Littlejohn took a sip of her coffee, giving Cynthia a chance to think about her response.

"No. Something and nothing, she told us. Married couples bicker all the time, especially when they're not at home, don't they?"

"Do you bicker with your husband whilst on holiday?" Littlejohn pressed.

"It was hardly a holiday. They were here for the weekend."

"What day did they arrive?"

Cynthia quickly supplied the answer. "Friday around six o'clock."

"And yet within twenty-four hours, the couple were arguing, which subsequently led to Callum Carter's death. Can you see where this line of questions is leading?"

"I can and I think you're wrong, Inspector. My interpretation is that it was a slight disagreement and they went their separate ways. Maybe Callum got disorientated and that led to his death. Oh, I'm not sure. It's hard to know what to think. It's awful knowing that he'll never walk through the door again. I dread to think how Reg is going to react once it truly sinks in. He's holding it together for Belinda's sake at present. We both are. Goodness me, what is this world coming to when a man chooses to take a walk on the beach and his life is ended just like that?" Cynthia snapped her finger and thumb together.

"You're sensing this is more than an accident by what you've just said, aren't you, Cynthia?" Ruth jumped in.

Her friend shook her head and fiddled with a wooden coaster on the kitchen table. "I don't know what to think. It's hard to get my thoughts into any semblance of order at this upsetting time. So please forgive me."

"There's nothing to forgive, you're understandably upset. I would be the same in your shoes if one of my friends had just lost their lives." Ruth reached across the table to grasp Cynthia's hand.

"I don't want your sympathy, Ruth, what I need is for you to find out the truth behind Callum's death. Do you think, between you, you'll be able to do that?"

"We're going to do our best," Littlejohn spoke for both of them. "Perhaps either Callum or Belinda mentioned something in passing that you think we should be aware of?"

Cynthia took a while to respond. "I've tried to think. I can't recall anything. I'm not surprised by that, though. Callum was always a man who appeared to put a brave face on things."

"Would you regard Belinda as being the same?" Ruth asked, already sensing what the answer was going to be.

"No. I couldn't say that. Maybe it would be best if you directed that question at her."

"We will do, just not today," Littlejohn replied. Lowering her voice a notch, she asked, "Do you know if they had any money troubles?"

"Again, I wouldn't like to say the wrong thing, so I'm going to keep quiet on that one as well."

Ruth turned to Littlejohn and shrugged. Where did they go from here?

Littlejohn closed her notebook and stood. "We'll leave it for now and come back another day to question Belinda. If you can emphasise to her how important it is for her to open up to us, that'll make my job a whole lot easier."

"I will," Cynthia said, nodding.

Ruth saw Littlejohn to the front door. They stopped off in the lounge to pick up Kenton en route. Belinda was still full of emotion whilst speaking to a relative on the phone. Reg was next to her, offering some comfort.

"Don't forget to keep in touch on this one, Miss Morgan, or should I call you Ruth now?"

Ruth shrugged. "Either or, I'm not bothered. I'll be leaving here soon myself. I'll ring you if I hear anything in the meantime." *Or will*

I? I'm still uncertain about you, Inspector. My suspicious mind and all that.

"Enjoy the rest of your weekend. We'll go back to the station and begin the investigation. We have a skeleton staff working today, but there's no time to lose on this one."

Kenton gave Ruth a brief nod, and they both left the house. Ruth closed the door behind them, and when she turned around, Cynthia was standing right behind her.

"Crikey! You almost gave me a heart attack."

"Sorry, Ruth. What do you make of her? She seemed more human than you've portrayed her to be in the past. Do you trust her?"

Ruth smiled at the way Cynthia always appeared to read her mind. "Truthfully, I'm not sure. I'll be cautious going forward. You know where I am if either you or Belinda need to speak or confide in me about something. I'm going to go home now. I have bridges of my own to build."

"You haven't fallen out with James, have you?"

"Not intentionally. He told me he was going home to pack a bag. Don't think my personal life will be detrimental to Callum's case, it won't. I'm professional enough to keep the two things separated."

Cynthia stepped forward with her arms open, and Ruth walked into them. "I'm here, too, if you ever want to chat about anything. I know your parents are travelling now. Don't think you can't confide in anyone."

"You're a good friend, Cynthia. I'll leave you to it. I'll give you a ring tonight…oops, it'll have to be after the am-dram club, if that's okay?"

"Of course it is. You enjoy yourself. I hope you can catch James before it's too late."

Ruth smiled, popped her head into the lounge to say cheerio to the others, and then left. First stop would have to be the park to give Ben some exercise. The poor thing must be on the verge of his bladder bursting. After a quick run around the park, Ruth bit the bullet and drove home. Entering the cottage sent a chill scampering up her spine. She held Ben's collar, forcing him to remain still, and tilted her head to listen. There was nothing to hear. The house was silent except for her ragged breath filling the hallway. She let go of Ben and followed her companion into the kitchen. He immediately went to his bowls, hinting that he was hungry. He lapped at his water and then glanced her way as if reminding her to feed him.

"As if I could ever forget to do that, boy. You'd never let me for a start." In her quest to avoid going upstairs to see if James had honoured his word by packing a bag and leaving for a few days, she busied herself in the kitchen, preparing not only Ben's dinner but something light for herself, too. A cheese and tomato omelette should fill the gap, not that she was that hungry. However, if she didn't eat now, she'd have little opportunity to do it later, what with attending the meeting this evening. She'd need to leave in an hour. That gave her enough time to prepare and eat her snack and tidy the kitchen up. Keeping her mind occupied would be the key to getting through this troubled spell and stopping her overthinking the situation with James.

He'd walked out on her, it was as simple as that. Other women would be in bits by now. Not Ruth, she was made of sterner stuff than that. Of course she would miss him, there was no doubting that, but at the end of the day they were two individuals still. Two people capable of making their own decisions. Whether those decisions were right or wrong, she wasn't sure. He was at his mate's house. If her feelings did prod her to do something about it, she knew where he was. She was sure about one thing: she wouldn't be calling him today as she was far too busy.

Really? I'm setting aside putting my relationship back on track to attend the usual meeting at the club? What does that tell me? Ten years I've been seeing that man. In that time, he's done nothing but nag me to get engaged. The minute he slips the ring on my finger and we have our first argument, he does a bunk.

She forced herself not to think things were permanently over between them. Their relationship had always been tempestuous over the years. They were both extremely stubborn and set in their ways. Every now and then that stubbornness showed itself and when that happened in the past, they'd dealt with it; there was no point in her thinking that this time would be any different.

After Ben ate his dinner, she let him out into the garden while she cooked her omelette in the heavy-based frying pan. Ruth sat at the kitchen table and toyed with her food, nibbling at the ingredients as if it had been concocted out of a bunch of insects, not enjoying the experience one iota. In the end, she pushed her plate away, her omelette three-quarters eaten. Refusing to sit there and dwell on things, she rang Steven.

"What time do you usually get to the community centre?"

"I open up around six forty-five. Why?"

"I'll see you then." She hung up, not giving him the chance to delve any deeper. She knew he'd grill her enough when she saw him in person later.

5

"*W*hat's this all about?" Steven demanded the instant he saw her.

She was already waiting outside the community centre when he showed up with the key.

"Wait, don't tell me now, let's get inside first out of this blasted weather. Have I mentioned lately how much I detest the British winters? This svelte body is built for reclining on sun loungers in exotic places, not battling hundred-mile-an-hour gusts of wind. I ended up on my backside in the gutter the other day. Legs akimbo right in front of a couple of hunky bodybuilders coming out of the gym. Not a pleasant experience, I can tell you."

Ruth sniggered. Same old Steven, ever the drama queen. A loveable character nevertheless and one of her dearest friends. "You always make me laugh."

"I sense your need. What's wrong, love?"

Ruth closed the door behind her and surprised both of them by breaking down.

Steven rushed to hug her, his hand smoothing the back of her head as she snuggled into his neck. "I'm sorry. I've been so strong. It wasn't my intention to burden you like this, Steven, not when you're only just getting over your ordeal."

"Nonsense, precious. My ordeal is in the past. Your situation is current and obviously causing you a lot of pain. Spill. No, wait, let's organise a cuppa first, and then you can tell me everything." He gently pushed her away and flew across the room where he filled the kettle and got two mugs ready. He was back with the coffee within a few minutes. He motioned for her to sit at the refectory-type table and pulled out the chair next to hers.

Ruth sat, suddenly feeling rather foolish.

"I know that look. I sense you're going to back out now that the time has arrived to reveal all. Don't. Tell me what's wrong or you and I, young lady, are going to fall out, big time. You hear me?"

"It's nothing compared to what you went through recently. I'll survive. I have to."

"Damn you, Ruth Morgan, get on with it and stop keeping me in suspenders. They hurt, you know, really uncomfortable, and rub the hairs on my legs."

She shook her head and grinned at him. "What would I do without you in my life to brighten the darkest of days?"

"I can't answer that. Come on, love, spill the beans."

"It's all gone wrong between me and James."

He launched himself back in his chair and placed a hand to his cheek. "Never. I don't believe you. You two are as solid as…oh God, I can't think of something damn solid to compare you to that wouldn't offend you."

"You're incorrigible. Why hasn't someone snapped you up by now?"

"Umm…don't you go getting any ideas now…you know you're the wrong gender for me. Anyway, I'm fussy with whom I share my sandwiches."

"You're adorable and a true friend. I don't know what's gone wrong. Maybe having the ring on my finger has cursed our relationship."

He tapped the side of his head. "It's all up here. You guys are always falling out. Having a ring on your finger was never going to change that. Don't go reading things into it that aren't there, princess. Why don't you tell me what's happened?"

She explained the way they'd fallen out when they'd got back to the car.

He took a swig of his coffee, contemplating his response. Eventually, he made a purr-like sound at the back of his throat. "You'll make it up. He's tetchy, that's all. His boss was there, and you sounded off, as usual." He raised a hand to prevent her from speaking. "Listen to me. He's the one who has to face her at work every day. You and I both know you despise the woman. Gosh, even I hate her after the way she treated me. The difference is, that I would choose to ignore her if she ever came anywhere near me, whereas you, my precious friend, tend to go for the jugular. Can you imagine how James must feel, stuck in the middle like that?"

"All right, I know I'm the one in the wrong. Anyway, Littlejohn and I have since agreed to work alongside each other on this case."

His eyebrows shot up. "You *have*? Do you intend sticking to that?"

She swivelled her mug on the table and tried to avoid his question for as long as she could.

He placed a finger under her chin and raised her eyes to look at him. "Ruth? Be honest with me?"

"It's going to be hard for me to relinquish my hold on a case which I've been employed by a friend to handle. I wouldn't have given up on you, so why should I give up on Callum's case?"

"You're terrible. Who said anything about 'relinquishing your hold' on the damn case? You've been asked to share information, so do it."

"Why should I? Why should I allow her to take the credit for a case I'm going to solve?"

"Who says you're going to solve it? The ball is in her court—she'll be privy to the post-mortem result long before you're going to get your grubby hands on it. Why do you have to make life difficult for yourself, Ruth? Do the right thing for all your sakes. And yes, that's me talking, the man she threw in a police cell and accused of murdering his idol. If I can forgive and forget, then you can do the same, can't you?"

She tilted her head back, heaved out a long sigh and twirled her mug again. "That's the trouble, you know how much of a control freak I am. It's tearing me in two to think I have to work with that woman, the same woman I've always regarded as my nemesis. Yes, she was the one to make the first move about sharing information. Maybe I'm doing her an injustice. I don't know, I'm confused and going out of my mind."

"It's not that dilemma that's driving you crazy, it's the fact that James has walked out on you, that's the real problem here."

"What? He hasn't?" Lynn Harris said behind them. They both leapt out of the chairs in fright.

Ruth and Steven had been that engrossed in their conversation neither of them had heard the door open. The rest of the group was standing next to Lynn, their expressions full of concern.

Lynn rushed to give Ruth a hug. "My God, girl, is that man mad? He must be to leave you."

"There are extenuating circumstances, but the crunch is that he's packed his bag and is staying with a friend for the next few days."

Lynn held up Ruth's left hand. "Things can't be that bad, otherwise you would have ripped your ring off and flung it at him, knowing you the way I do."

Ruth offered a weak smile. "You're right. Let's hope that's the case anyway."

"Dare I ask why he's walked out?" Hilary asked, giving Ruth's arm a sympathetic stroke.

"Over the case I'm working on."

"Ooo…is it another murder case?" Hilary shot Steven an apologetic look which he batted away with his hand.

"We're not sure yet. Why don't you guys sort yourselves out a drink and we'll have a natter about it? Don't worry about me, I'll be fine. James will come home when he feels he's punished me enough. You know what men are like when their pride is dented."

The group wandered over to the refreshment area and left Steven with Ruth.

He leaned forward and whispered, "I'm so sorry. I'm not sure you wanted the news to be spread like that."

"It's fine. They would have found out sooner or later."

The group rejoined them at the long table. The atmosphere was kind of subdued. Ruth hated that. The thing she loved most about Sunday nights was the enthusiasm everyone exuded whilst at the club.

She clapped to gain everyone's attention. "Guys, please, don't let my circumstances sour the evening. If I was that upset about my position then I would have stayed at home with Ben, drowning my sorrows in a large G&T. We have a lot of preparations to still attend to for our next production, don't we? Maybe you'd care to start things off, Steven?"

He nodded and squeezed her hand. Ever the professional, Ruth was determined that tonight would be a success. Life went on. Hurdles sprang up in everyone's life. It was how you sprinted over them that mattered.

Once Steven had brought them all up to date and he'd given each of them a task to perform, the conversation turned to what Ruth had mentioned at the beginning of the evening—her new case. While everyone was there, she said, "So that's where things stand at present. I don't suppose anyone was out last night and saw this chappie heading towards the beach, did they?"

Everyone shook their head bar Hilary.

"What's wrong, Hils?"

"Something is pricking my mind, and I can't think what it is. Leave me alone to think about it for a second or two."

"Of course."

Lynn raised her hand to speak. "So, are you saying this was intentional, Ruth?"

"I can't say that yet, Lynn, not until we hear back from the pathologist on that one."

"Funny they should have an argument and then she took off for home without him, isn't it?" Gemma asked.

"It is what it is, Gem."

"Would you walk off in a strange town without telling your spouse where you were going?" Gemma probed.

Ruth had to admit she wouldn't, and it was something that hadn't sat well with her from the outset. "I can't say I would. But before we start casting aspersions, we don't know all the facts as to why they argued. It's best if we don't speculate or judge the couple for having what apparently was a little spat."

"A little spat which has ended in someone's death. Come off it, Ruth, that's hard to fathom for anyone, not just the local police or a paid private investigator," Hilary stated.

"I'm not trying to make excuses for the wife here, I promise. I have my doubts, only by the second-hand information I've received about the woman from my friend, Cynthia. I don't intend to let that cloud my judgement on the case. Hils, have you thought about what was niggling you?"

"I have. The only thing I can suggest is asking my friend, Lydia Belmont, if she saw anything at the beach. She takes a stroll down there with her dog, Titus, at least four times a day. I'll ring her and get back to you, if that's all right?"

"Excellent news. I know Lydia, I haven't spoken to her in years, not sure if she'll remember me. Can you do that for me this evening, if it's not too much trouble?"

"I'll do it now, if nobody else minds?"

Everyone sitting around the table cheered Hilary on and fell silent when she connected with Lydia.

"You did? Oh my...yes...no...I can't say much. Look, Lydia, a friend of mine, Ruth Morgan, is investigating the case and is keen to have a chat with you. Would you be up for that? No, she's not a nosy parker, she's a private investigator who is exceptional at her job... you're amazing." Hilary looked up from the table she'd been staring at and raised her thumb at Ruth. "Tomorrow? Okay, what time suits you best...? The earlier the better, if you would. Ruth is an extremely busy lady. Wonderful, okay, ten it is. I'll give her your address. Thanks for helping out like this, Lydia." Hilary ended the call and punched the air.

"Well?" Ruth demanded impatiently.

"She saw a man at the beach," Hilary replied, nodding slowly.

"Really? Okay, well, that sounds intriguing. Thanks for giving me an in with your friend, Hils."

"Let me know what she tells you. I feel invested in this case now."

"I will. I can see Steven giving me the evil eye. We'd better get down to club business, otherwise he's likely to lynch me."

"I would never do such a thing, you're far too valuable to the community, Miss Private Investigator Extraordinaire."

"You're too kind." Ruth's cheeks warmed up under everyone's gaze and nods of approval at his statement.

The rest of the evening consisted of Steven going through all the outfits and props he'd sourced for the production. Ruth loved the era *Guys and Dolls* was set in. The fashion back then was far better than any recent era, in her book anyway. She couldn't wait to play dress-up.

The evening drew to a close. The other members drifted off, leaving Ruth alone with Steven once more.

"You handled the evening well, considering what's going on at home," he said, collecting the mugs from the table and depositing them on the draining board for Ruth to wash.

"Life goes on, as you know only too well. Why dwell on matters that are totally out of your hands?"

"Are they? Out of your hands? All it would take is a sincere chat with your other half, and I have no doubt you guys could put your differences aside and get on with your lives. If that's what you really want, Ruth, is it?"

She sighed, washed up the final mug and placed it on the draining board for him to wipe. "I'm having second thoughts about the engagement. Maybe I was right saying no to his proposals all those years."

"No way! You two are solid."

She raised an eyebrow. "We've split up. How can you say that, Steven?"

"Easily. From an outsider's point of view, you two are as solid as any couple celebrating their fiftieth wedding anniversary. You've hit a large bump in an otherwise smooth road in recent weeks. Don't let it alter the way you feel about him, princess. Admit it, you still love him, right?"

"Of course I do. I couldn't fall out of love with him as easily as that. It's the pressure of having a damn ring on my finger that I can't handle."

"Then stop wearing it. It's an immaterial object." He punched a fist against his chest a few times. "It's what's in here that counts, not the confounded status of flashing an engagement ring off. You, my dear girl, should be above doing what others expect of you and do what's right for you and James."

"He's the one who has hounded me for years to marry him or get engaged and now he's the one who has ended up running out on me." She swallowed down the lump that had suddenly emerged in her throat.

Steven stepped forward and gathered her in his arms.

She pushed away from him. "Don't be kind to me, you'll turn me into a crumbling wreck."

"If you want me to slap you around the face and tell you how foolish you're being, I'd happily oblige."

She smiled through her tears. "You're a wonderful pal, Steven Swanson. I'm lucky to have you and all the others in my life. It is richer for it."

"James should feature in that sentiment, too, lovely lady. He loves, adores and cherishes you. Don't lose sight of that while you're struggling to get a handle on things. Promise me?"

"I won't. Maybe I'm guilty of doing that. I'll give myself a good talking-to when I get home. Let's face it, going back to an empty house, except for Ben being there, of course, is going to allow me the time to reflect and possibly put things back into perspective. After all, we fell out about my work. It wasn't as if we argued about anything personal."

"There you are, it sounds to me like you're already on the right track to solving your problems. Ring me later if you need to chat. I don't tend to hit the sack until midnight."

"I'll be in bed long before that. Whether I'll be able to sleep is a different matter, one that I'm not looking forward to pursuing."

He placed a hand against her cheek. His touch wrapped her in a warm blanket. "It's not like you to be so negative, sweetie. Negativity is bad for the soul, it eats away at you, I should know. Come on, let all that pent-up emotion out. Copy me." He took a few paces back and shook his arms out in front of him and then took them out to the sides and finished off raising them above his head. "Feel all that tension seeping away."

She felt foolish following his lead but did it all the same, surprised to find out that his statement was indeed true. A few moments of shaking her body from top to toe made her feel a lot better about herself. She smiled. "You're a genius."

He snorted. "Hardly. I do it all the time to relieve stress at work. You have no idea how stressed I get dealing with the little terrors in the community."

"I can imagine," she replied, smiling. She leaned forward and hugged him again, feeling better in herself now she'd shared her woes with him. "Thanks for listening."

"My pleasure. I'm always available day and night for a chat, you know that, princess. Come on, I'll switch off the lights and walk out with you."

"Do you need a lift home? The weather is still foul out there by the sounds of it."

"No, I'm fine. I need to blow the cobwebs out of my brain and get ready for the day job tomorrow. It's what I do on a weekly basis, every Sunday after the meet-up. Enjoy the rest of your evening, give Ben a cuddle from me. And stop worrying, things will sort themselves out. I'm confident they will."

"I wish I could say the same. Thanks for the pep talk, Steven. Goodnight." She kissed his cheek and rushed through the drizzle to Betty. "Don't let me down now, girl."

Luckily, the car started on the first turn of the ignition. She waved to Steven and drew away. Driving back to the cottage, which was a stone's throw away, she couldn't help letting her mind wander back to the falling out she'd had with James. She parked Betty outside her home and entered the house, all the while trying to make sense of it all. She hadn't changed since they'd become engaged but she sensed he had, a little. How? She couldn't quite put her finger on that for now. Ben was there to greet her. She got down on her haunches, nuzzled into his fur and found it hard to prevent the damn tears cascading down her cheeks again. He licked at their saltiness and moaned against her ear, sensing her mood as he was always adept at doing.

"I'm fine. It's better out than in, as my old nan used to say. Oops, no, upon reflection, I think she was talking about her bouts of wind when she said that." Ruth laughed at her mistake and went through to the kitchen to let Ben out in the garden. With the back door wedged open with the bin, in case the wind got up and slammed it shut, she poured herself a glass of wine. As she waited for Ben to reappear, she contemplated phoning James, if only to hear his voice. She bypassed the idea pretty darn quickly, though, not liking the fact that she should be the one to back down and apologise, especially as, in her eyes, she'd done nothing wrong.

She ended up snuggling up to Ben on the couch for a couple of hours and, before long, she realised she'd finished a whole bottle of wine and her head was muzzy as hell. "Time for bed, Ben."

The drink had done the trick. She didn't even recall getting undressed and, as soon as her head sank into the pillow, she fell asleep.

6

The following morning, Ruth downed a couple of paracetamol along with her coffee and toast. It was gone nine when she'd finally opened her eyes. In her haste to get in the shower, she forgot about the wine she'd drunk the previous evening and almost landed up on her backside on the bedroom carpet when her legs lacked coordination with her brain. She couldn't still be drunk, could she?

No way. I've drunk far more wine than that in the past and been perfectly okay the next day. Maybe there was something extra in the bottle. Is that possible? Or is it my mind playing tricks on me?

She battled on regardless, and by the time she'd showered and got dressed, she felt almost human again. Ben was standing by his dish in the kitchen when she went downstairs. "Hungry are you, Munchkin?"

He moaned a reply and tapped his dish with his paw.

She fed him, washed up her breakfast plate and mug, and then left the house with Ben. First stop, a run around the park for her four-legged companion. She pulled up and was surprised to see Cynthia there with Roxy.

"Hi, I didn't expect to see you here today."

Cynthia turned to face her and Ruth immediately noticed the red rings around her friend's eyes. She flew over and gave her a hug.

"My goodness, Cynthia, whatever is the matter? Silly me, ignore that trite remark. How dumb of me not to think you'd still be upset by Callum's death."

Cynthia waved her concern away. "It's not that. Have you ever felt like you're a stranger in your own home?"

Ruth shook her head. "I'm sorry you feel like that. All this must be hard on both you and Reg. After all the renovations you've had to contend with in recent months, this is not what you need at all."

"It's what is about to happen that worries me, not what's gone on before."

Keeping one eye on what Ben was up to and the other on Cynthia, she asked, "What on earth do you mean?"

The wind had swept up a clump of Cynthia's grey hair, she sighed and tucked it behind her left ear. "After you left yesterday, Belinda spent the next few hours calling everyone and their dog to share the awful news. I thought that would be the end of it—I was wrong. Throughout the evening, I must have answered the phone half a dozen times. Each time it was for Belinda—annoying in itself that they didn't contact her on her mobile; however, the outcome is that all these people are going to descend on us over the next few days."

"Descend how? Not come and stay with you?"

"I didn't have the heart to say no. We haven't got enough beds for all of them. Reg is out there now, sourcing temporary beds, as in camp beds, sleeping bags et cetera."

"No. You can't be expected to put these people up, Cynthia. Tell them to book into the hotel instead."

Cynthia's head dropped, and she kicked out at the soggy leaves underfoot. "I don't have it in me to tell them to do that. I'd look a monster in their eyes, wouldn't I?"

"No way. Of course you wouldn't. Gosh, I wish I could help out. I'm with you, though, I'd loathe letting total strangers stay in my house. You should ring the hotel, get them to offer you a special rate and let Belinda's family stay there."

Cynthia smiled and nodded. "I knew there would be an obvious solution. I'm indebted to you once more, Ruth."

"Nonsense, you would have thought about it eventually." She glanced at her watch—it was ten minutes to ten. "Heck, I'm going to be late for my first appointment. Sorry to have to love you and run out on you, Cynthia."

"Not a problem, you're a busy lady. Does this have any bearing on the investigation, dare I ask?"

"Possibly. I'll fill you in later. Ben, come on, boy, back in the car."

Ben stopped flirting with Roxy and came the instant he was called.

"Take care, ring me soon, Ruth," Cynthia shouted after her.

"I will. I promise. Do the right thing for your own peace of mind and tell those imminent guests of yours to do one."

"Okay, I'll tell them you told me to kick them out. Drive safely."

They both laughed.

"That'll go down well, I'm sure."

Ruth buckled Ben into the back seat and started up Betty, who annoyed her by being a little slow to get going this morning. She bashed the steering wheel with her clenched fist. "Come on, Betty, don't let me down now, girl."

The car sparked into life and spat out a plume of smoke from the exhaust. "Great, just what I need. I'd better drop by Pat's garage later, see if he'll work his magic on you. I can't have you letting me down at an inopportune moment." She tentatively pulled away from the kerb, and when Betty responded, if a little hesitantly at first, Ruth let out a relieved sigh.

Five minutes later, she drew up outside Lydia Belmont's cute two-bed terraced house. Lydia must have been looking out for her because she appeared in the doorway before Ruth had even stepped foot on the front path.

"Nice to see you, Ruth, it's been a while."

They hugged. "How are things? I take it you haven't found another job yet?"

"Not yet. I was pleased when the firm closed down and gave me the redundancy package. I'm frugal with my money, so it's no great hardship to live off what's left for a little while. In truth, I'm enjoying spending more time at home with Titus."

"I'd be lost without Ben as my constant companion at the office all day. It's surprising how reliant we become on them, isn't it? Breaks my heart to think of the many dogs out there, forced to stay at home all day by themselves. All they want is companionship and to know that they're loved...Oh gosh, here I go... Listen to me!"

"No, you're entitled to your opinion, and yes, I think you're one hundred percent right. When I do eventually search for a new job, I'll be going part-time. Better still, it would be wonderful if I found a job I could do from home, then I needn't leave her alone ever again."

"Those types of jobs are few and far between. Good luck with that."

"Enough about me. Come in. Fancy a coffee?"

"That would be wonderful. Another nippy day ahead of us by the look of things." Ruth followed Lydia through the house to the tiny kitchen at the rear, full of dated pine units.

"Take a seat. White coffee with sugar?"

"Just the ticket. Hello, Titus, how are you doing?" Titus the boxer snuffled around at her feet, sat in front of her and offered her paw for Ruth to shake. "I see her manners are impeccable as ever."

Lydia chuckled and finished fixing the drinks. "She's a sweetheart. I've noticed a difference in her since I've been home."

"Just goes to show how much they thrive when they're part of the pack."

"It does. Anyway, enough about us. How's business? I've always admired the way you tackle your work. You always seem to be rushed off your feet. Who'd have thought a small town like this would have so much crime?"

"Ha ha, well, it's a little quiet at present, so I suppose the natives are learning to behave themselves. Actually, correct that, it was quiet until this new case landed in my lap. Hence my visit. Did Hilary fill you in?"

"Yes, briefly. I also heard the gossip flying around. If Hils hadn't told you, I would have rung you myself within a day or two."

"Glad to hear it. Awful business. Can you tell me what you saw?"

"Rightio, it feels good to know my information might help catch a criminal."

Ruth raised her hand in front of her. "Let's not get carried away just yet."

"Sorry. I've always been guilty of letting my enthusiasm get the better of me. I took Titus for her usual walk along the beach on Saturday evening. I know I shouldn't be down there by myself at night, especially at this time of year now that the weather is bleak. Try telling that to this one. I head up the other way to the park, and she insists on dragging me in the opposite direction. She's so strong, I don't have it in me to argue with her. Oh dear, I'm chuntering on, you don't want to hear all that. Anyway, we set off around five-thirty, intending to be out for half an hour, that's all. Titus had other ideas, though, and once she was on the beach, prancing around like an Arabian horse, well, I didn't have it in my heart to drag her back home again too soon."

"I think all dog owners would think the same, Lydia."

A frown developed on her face. "I could name a few in this town who'd be inclined to disagree with us on that one. Not naming anyone because I'm not a snitch, but I've cringed a few times recently when I've seen a couple of the owners treating their dogs...roughly, shall we say."

"No. Oh gosh, I hate to see any kind of animal abuse. Did you say anything?"

"I couldn't. It's difficult living alone. You're always fearing some kind of reprisal if you even look at a person in the wrong way." She shuddered, and Ruth reached over and patted her on the hand.

"Don't feel guilty. If you're that concerned for the dogs, why don't you place an anonymous call to the RSPCA?"

Lydia perked up at the suggestion. "I never thought about doing that. I'll ring them today. Hate the thought of those dogs living their lives in fear."

"Oh my, that bad?"

"Maybe I'm guilty of exaggerating a little. Anyway, back to my story, I know how busy you are. The last thing I want to do is hold you up."

"Take your time."

"Titus was running and barking a lot. Even though it was a gusty night, she could still be heard. I called her a few times. At first, she ignored me. I usually stay on the edge of the beach, on the promenade there; we play fetch most of the time. Not on Saturday. It was as though she'd been taken over by an alien being." She laughed. "What am I like? Yes, that was another one of my slight embellishments. I called and called her, and she kept barking. Although the promenade was lit, the main reason I stay there while she runs her heart out, the beach was pitch-black. She was bothering me, so I ventured onto the beach. It was tricky getting down there. I followed her bark and finally found her. I was just attaching her leash when out of the blue a man wearing a hood stumbled into me. He mumbled an apology, we both did, and he went on his way. I was getting ready to leave the beach and set off after him. The whole time he walked he kept looking over his shoulder at me. I felt a tad self-conscious, not scared—it was a weird feeling. Once I heard about that poor man's death, I shuddered. I'm not generally a suspicious person as a rule, Ruth, but I swear that man who bumped into me, well, I think he's the one."

"The one?"

"Who did that poor man a mischief."

Ruth tutted. "Well, here's our dilemma at present: until the post-mortem results come back, we can't say if foul play was involved or not."

"But I'm telling you I saw a man, a suspicious-looking one at that, down there on the beach that night. Doesn't that count for anything?"

"It might do, depending on the results. I'm working with the police on this case. I'll be sure to let them know what you saw."

"Will I have to give a statement?" she asked, frowning.

"Most definitely. Although, we have to bear in mind that the weather was bad that night, and just because the person had his hood up, he could still be innocent. We mustn't get too carried away."

Lydia glanced down at her mug as if mortally offended. "I know what I saw, though, Ruth."

"Lydia, I believe you. I'm just sitting back and taking things cautiously. It was definitely a man you saw, though, yes?"

"Oh yes, there is no doubt in my mind about that."

"If the police asked you to give them a formal ID or got you to search through their database for the possible suspect, would you be able to do that?"

Lydia paused and scratched the side of her head. "I suppose so. Heck, I'm only trying to help, and look what a muddle I'm in already. I wish I'd kept my mouth shut now."

"Don't be like that. You'd rather it was me saying all this than the police, wouldn't you?"

"I suppose so."

Ruth sipped at her drink, which was still piping hot and contemplated what her next move should be. *Should I ring Littlejohn? Will she be ticked off with me if this is all Lydia can tell us?*

"What's going on in that head of yours?"

"Sorry, I was miles away. I'm going to ring the inspector I'm working with and get her advice on this one. Excuse me a second. All right if I go in the garden?"

"No, you stay here in the warm. I'll busy myself in the lounge. Give me a shout when you're done."

Ruth smiled and watched Lydia leave the room, delaying the phone call she knew she had to make. Gulping down a few lungfuls of air, she braced herself and tapped in the station's number. "DI Littlejohn, please, it's urgent," she told the girl on the switchboard.

"Just a moment. I'll see if she's available to take your call, madam. Who shall I say is calling?"

"I'm Ruth Morgan, she'll want to speak to me."

"Thank you for your patience."

The line fell silent until an abrupt Littlejohn came on. "Miss Morgan, what can I do for you?"

"I'm at a local's house. She was walking on the beach the night Callum Carter died."

"And?" Littlejohn rudely interrupted her.

"And, I think she might have something that could be relevant to the investigation."

"How so?"

Ruth clenched and unclenched her free hand. "She was walking her dog, and someone wearing a hood bumped into her."

"That doesn't mean a thing. It could be a coincidence. The fact the person was wearing a hood is neither here nor there, given the weather that evening."

"I know that. I still think it's worth taking a statement from her. Maybe even use her to try and obtain a description of the man?"

"Maybe. Okay, I'm willing to do it this time. I'll send one of our men over to have a chat. Give me the woman's name and address?"

Ruth reeled the details off, and Littlejohn hung up, leaving Ruth seething and furious she'd shared the information in the first place. *What is that damn woman's problem? She tells me she wants to share details, and when I do... Grr... Maybe I should reconsider our agreement, lady, see how you respond to that news.*

"Lydia, you can come back in now."

Lydia and Titus entered the room again. "How did you get on?"

"The inspector asked me to pass on her thanks and said that she was going to send one of her team out to take a statement from you." The first half was a lie, Ruth knew that.

Lydia nodded. "Okay, is it normal to feel scared with the thought of the police showing up at my door?"

"Not at all. They're normal human beings, simply doing their job."

"Scary all the same," she replied, smiling weakly.

Ruth finished her drink and rose from the table. "You'll be fine. I can't tell you how much I personally appreciate hearing what you had to say. I'm sure the officer, when he arrives, will feel the same way. Good luck, not that you'll need it, and thanks for the coffee."

"You're welcome." Lydia showed her to the front door, Titus panting at her heel. "Will I have time to walk Titus?"

"I should think so. Can you go now? I doubt the inspector will be able to organise anything for an hour or two."

"I'll fetch my coat and set off. Thanks for stopping by, Ruth. I hope your investigation goes well."

"Me, too. See you soon." Ruth closed the front door behind her.

She strolled back to the car, lost in thought. Ben slipped his head between the seats and licked her cheek as she got in. "Cheeky. I know what you're after. I have an idea, call it a reconnaissance mission. Let's go down to the beach. Hopefully it'll be open to the residents again by now."

He groaned, his pleasure recognisable, and settled back into his seat. Ruth drove the short distance and was relieved to see the promenade and the beach were both clear of crime scene tape. She unhooked Ben from his harness and motioned for him to come to heel. They wandered down the promenade and onto the stony beach, heading for the sandier part to go easier on Ben's paws.

During the stroll, Ruth ran through what Lydia had told her and picked out a likely spot where the man had bumped into her. In her head, she measured the distance between the rock where Callum's body was discovered and the area she was standing in. It was around a hundred feet, give or take. *Hmm...plausible indeed. Although, if I had just committed a crime, the last thing I would have done was come back on the beach. I would've continued along the rocks at the rear.*

Ben barked at her side, breaking into her thoughts. She picked up a large stone and hurled it ahead of her. "Fetch it, boy."

He charged after the stone and retrieved it. Instead of bringing it straight back to her, he got distracted and began sniffing at the sand. Then he pawed at the beach. Intrigued, Ruth went to investigate. To her disappointment, it turned out to be a crab burrowing itself into the sand. "Leave the poor thing alone, monkey. How would you like it if a giant came along and messed with your house?" She pulled on his collar and threw another stone in the opposite direction to distract him.

He bounded after it, giving her a moment to think over the events of Saturday night, what there were of them. Who was this hooded man? Did he have an agenda? Was he known to Callum Carter? Was this person a local? A person on the rob? No, as far as she knew, Callum hadn't had anything taken, although she'd need to check that aspect with Littlejohn. Again, she was left with far more questions than answers, and it was driving her nuts, even though she was aware of how frustrating a new case could be at times.

After running Ben ragged for the next fifteen minutes, she decided it would be best to return to Cynthia's to see if Belinda was up for a chat. If not, then she was stumped on how to proceed.

"Ben, come on, boy. Time to go back to the car."

He laid down on the sand until she got close to him, then he walked to heel back up the beach and onto the promenade where the car was parked. She removed his dish and a bottle of water she filled every morning from the garden tap and waited patiently for him to lap up all the contents. After securing him in the back seat, she fired up Betty once more. The old banger turned over a few times and then surprised her by starting on the third attempt, just when she'd given up all hope on the old girl coming through for her. She revved the engine a few more times and then drove off. Ruth stopped off at Pat's garage on the way through town.

He was pleased to see her and came to greet her, wiping his hands on an oily rag. "Hello, Ruth. Don't tell me your folks have broken down again!"

She held her crossed fingers up in the air. "I haven't heard from them since you rescued them, so I'm presuming they're enjoying their stay up in Scotland."

"Good to hear. What can I do for you then?"

She pointed at her faithful chariot. "It's her. She's suffering on these cold mornings."

"I know how that feels. My old bones are making it harder for me to get out of bed every morning. Do you want me to have a quick peek under the bonnet for you and give my expert opinion?"

"Would you?"

He opened the bonnet and made a lot of *hmm* noises.

She couldn't stand it any longer and urged, "What's the prognosis? Will she survive another few months at least?"

He closed the bonnet and folded his arms. "I won't know until we get her up on the ramp. I couldn't see anything obvious going on under the bonnet. Can you leave her with me for a few days?"

"I could; however, that would leave me without a vehicle, and I'm in the middle of an investigation."

He winked at her. "We can't have our very own Miss Marple vehicle-less. I can sort out a courtesy car for you, if that'll help?"

"Would you? That would be wonderful. Ah, one problem…I have Ben to consider, and he moults significantly, no matter what time of year it is. I promise to clean the car before I return it to you."

He laughed. "If you do that, you'll be the first person ever to return the car cleaner than when it went out. Get away with you, I don't mind a few dog's hairs. I'm aware he's your constant companion. It's nice to see. I bring my German Shephard, Cara, to work. She's in the office sleeping at the moment. Better than leaving them at home all day, eh?"

"I couldn't agree more. Thanks, Pat, I appreciate you getting me out of this sticky situation."

"Nonsense. All in a day's work. We'll give her a mini service, change the oil and spark plugs. I'm guessing that'll be all that's needed. Don't quote me on that, though."

"I hope so, the bank balance couldn't stand anything major. I'll be looking at changing her as soon as I have funds available." She added the final part in a whisper in case Betty heard her.

Pat tapped the side of his nose. "Let me know if I can be of assistance in that department."

"I'll definitely stop by once the need arises."

He drove Betty into the service bay—she started first time for him, the cantankerous mare. He returned holding out the keys to a shiny black Ford fiesta.

Ruth collected her handbag and Ben's bits and pieces from Betty and put them in the new car, thanked Pat for saving her bacon and drove off.

Not sure where to go or what to do next for the best, she headed to Cynthia's house to possibly lend a hand with all that lay ahead of her with the imminent arrival of her guests.

Cynthia seemed pleased to see her standing on the front doorstep.

"Come in. Gosh, it's raining again. That wasn't in the forecast this morning when I checked. Glad we both managed to take the dogs out first thing. Any news? Is that a new car you have there?"

Ruth smiled. Cynthia didn't miss a thing. She explained about Betty and stepped into the house. Lowering her voice, she asked, "Thought I'd drop by to see if I could help with anything."

"You're too kind, Ruth. The first guest has arrived."

"Who is it?" she enquired, straining her neck muscles as she peered past Cynthia into the lounge.

"Gerald Rattner, he's Belinda's ex-husband."

Ruth shook her head in disbelief. "Wow, seriously? I'm not sure my ex would be at the top of my list to call if my current husband had just died."

Cynthia shrugged. "I thought the same. Tread carefully, Ruth, he's…how shall I say this…? Ah yes, a tad overprotective of her."

"Why? She's amongst friends here, isn't she? Don't answer that, it was a rhetorical question." It didn't stop her enquiring why all the same internally.

"You'll see once you've met him. Do you want a coffee?"

"You read my mind. Thanks, Cynthia, I'll never say no."

"Come with me, I'll introduce you and then make the drinks. I'm sure everyone will want another cuppa by now. He's been here about an hour or so. I'm dying to hear what you think of him."

Ruth frowned. "Sounds ominous."

Cynthia waved the suggestion away. "Not at all. You'll see what I mean."

She followed Cynthia into the lounge. "Gerald, this is my dear friend, Ruth Morgan. She's the town's private investigator and she's agreed to work on Callum's case for me. Ruth, this is Gerald Rattner, Belinda's ex-husband."

Ruth swept past Cynthia with an outstretched hand. Gerald stared at her hand as if it were laden with toxic germs. She dropped her arm to her side and studied the man in defiance, mirroring the way he seemed to be studying her.

"And what have you gathered so far in your investigation, Miss

Morgan?" His eyes narrowed to tiny slits, the wrinkles to the side telling Ruth he was older than she'd first thought.

"In truth, nothing much as yet. I'm working with the local police."

"Good. My advice would be to leave it to them to solve this riddle. They're the ones with all the knowledge and experience under their belts." His tone was abrupt and to the point.

"Meaning, I don't. Is that what you're inferring, Mr Rattner?" She took an instant dislike to this man for some reason and wasn't about to hold back. Men who openly put others down in public rattled her cage.

"Ruth has a great deal of experience, Gerald. She has solved the last two major crimes in Carmel Cove, long before the police had even started their investigation," Cynthia chipped in.

"Thank you, Cynthia. That's right, Mr Rattner, you see, being a local, and one who is well respected in the community, does have its benefits, in that the residents tend to confide in me more than they do in the officious local inspector." She cursed herself for snapping at the man.

He appeared to be too stunned to add a rebuttal, for now.

Cynthia bustled out of the room and into the kitchen. Ruth decided to go with her rather than stand there being observed by a man who had clearly mistrusted her.

"That was awkward. I apologise for snapping in there."

Cynthia closed the kitchen door and returned to her position to prepare the cups. "You don't have to apologise to me, dear, he got what was coming to him. Speaking to him since he arrived, I get the impression he's part of the old-school brigade. You know the type, women have a place in the home and not at the workplace. It showed, didn't it?"

"Why would Belinda put up with someone like that? I know she divorced him and moved on to Callum, but what I meant was, his type would be the last person I called after the death of my husband."

Cynthia nodded and loaded the tray with a milk jug, sugar bowl and a plate of biscuits. "I'm inclined to agree with you, but then, I always do. Don't let any man put you down, Ruth, you've got a good man in that fiancé of yours. He allows you to do far more than other men his age would."

"You think? I still get days when I believe James tries to suppress my input in things, either in my working life or around the house."

"You might think he does, but believe me, when you compare him to a man like Rattner, your James is an absolute angel. Have you noticed Reg hasn't said a word yet? He won't—he daren't open his mouth because he'll let Gerald know exactly what he thinks of him."

"He's not staying here if he's causing this much upset, is he?"

"Definitely not. I bit the bullet after chatting with you earlier and had a quiet word with Belinda. I said there's no way we'd be able to put everyone up who is due to descend on us. I thought she'd kick off but she appears to have accepted that I'm right. Told me that she would call the local hotel and arrange the rooms for her guests."

"That must be a huge relief for you, to be getting your house back?"

"We'll be halfway there, Belinda will still be staying with us, so there's no chance for us to relax and put our feet up again just yet."

"How's she taking Callum's death?"

Cynthia held her hand out and waved it from side to side. "So-so, I guess. One minute she's talking about him and the fond memories they have shared over the years, the next, she's bawling her eyes out with tears of anger spilling onto her cheeks. I suppose that's her grief showing."

"Possibly." Ruth leaned in closer and whispered, "Give me an honest answer, Cynthia. You don't think she's capable of killing Callum, do you?"

Cynthia stopped what she was doing, rested her back against the worktop and folded her arms. "I've been taking a leaf out of your book and studying her since his body was discovered and, in all honesty, I'm finding her impossible to read. Let's just say, if Reg died tomorrow, no one would be getting any sense out of me for a few days. Her grief is different to anyone else I've stumbled across. I know I shouldn't read much into that." She shrugged. "I don't know, I could be talking a lot of rubbish. Any news on the post-mortem yet?"

"I haven't heard anything. It's out of my hands, not something I have access to, so no chance of me chasing it up. I'm hoping Littlejohn sticks to her word and rings me as soon as she obtains the results. We can't really begin the investigation as such until then. Don't worry, I won't bill you for any wasted time, I promise."

"Don't say that. I'm not bothered about the money side of things. I know you well enough by now. Your integrity is second to none, that's why I like you so much, Ruth. I don't generally take to strangers as quickly as I've taken to you."

"That's lovely to hear. Thank you, it means a lot."

The kettle finished boiling, and Cynthia did the necessary to complete the drinks. "Ready to face the music again?" she asked, picking up the wooden tray.

"I'm ready. Let me get the door for you." Ruth pulled open the door and allowed Cynthia to go ahead of her. She inhaled a large breath, ready to go into battle with Gerald if the necessity arose.

Over drinks, everyone made small talk. Ruth caught Gerald staring at her over his cup a few times as he drank. His constant appraisal of her made her feel uncomfortable. After everyone had finished their drinks, Ruth gathered the cups and saucers, insisting Cynthia sit where she was, and took the tray into the kitchen where she proceeded to wash up. She heard footsteps behind her and then a gruff voice close to her ear.

"You're wasting your time, and Cynthia's money come to that, carrying on with your investigation. Why don't you leave it to the police?"

Ruth spun around quickly to find Gerald mere inches away from her. She felt intimidated and out of her comfort zone. Even dealing with the current crop of murderers she'd brought to justice hadn't made her feel as uncomfortable as he did. She dodged out of his way and picked up the tea towel hanging on the handle of the oven. "Excuse me? You've obviously got a problem with me, Mr Rattner, and yet you barely know me. Is there something you'd like to get off your chest?"

He took a few paces towards her, and she stumbled back against the chair. "You'll do best to stop snooping into what doesn't concern you. I've met your type before, a great number of times, in fact, and nothing good has come of meddlesome PIs butting their noses into an investigation."

Refusing to let him win, she stood erect, shoulders pinned back, her spine straight, and said, "Maybe you've come across some bad PIs in the past. Please don't tar us all with the same brush. I'm the ultimate professional, Mr Rattner. My experience and record speak for themselves if you'd care to look me up."

"Opinions can be bought. Friends are hardly going to slate you, are they, Miss Morgan?" he sneered.

His tone sent a shiver racing up her spine. *No matter what I say, I'm getting the impression this guy is set in his ways and isn't about to back down. I refuse to let him bully me like this. I have to call his bluff.*

"Am I to believe you were in the police force, Mr Rattner?"

"I was. I made it to the rank of detective sergeant in my career—with the Met, I hasten to add. The crème de la crème in the UK. Any idea how many PIs have set up down in London? *Thousands,* and I abhor the lot of them. Taking money from the most vulnerable in our society. Leading these unfortunate people astray. Stringing cases out just so they get paid extra—"

Ruth held up a hand to cut him off. "Comparing me with people such as those is disrespectful in itself. I wish you'd give me a chance to prove myself before thinking badly of me."

He grunted. "You're not the first to have said that to me either. You're all the same. Money-grabbing so-and-sos, who believe their own hype."

"That's grossly unfair of you, Mr Rattner. I'm upset you should think like that having only met me twenty minutes ago."

He shrugged. "Show me something you've done in this case to try and change my mind then?"

"That's difficult right now. You're aware, as well as I am, that when a death is undefined, there are procedures to follow. I'm waiting in line until certain results reach me."

"Leave it to the local police to deal with and stop interfering, preventing them from doing their jobs, you hear me?"

Standing tall once more, she shook her head. "It's not going to happen. Cynthia has employed me to find out the truth and that's what I intend to do. Maybe you'd care to answer a few questions for me? I'm confused as to why you're here actually. Why is that?"

"Not that this concerns you, but Belinda needed me to be here."

"An ex-partner? May I ask why you got divorced in the first place?"

"You can ask, doesn't mean I have to tell you. That's our personal business and has no bearing on this case."

"As you wish. I'm in contact with the local inspector and I'm reporting to her daily. I will be passing on details of the people who Belinda has invited, shall we say. Therefore, don't be surprised if the police pay you a visit in the next day or two."

His eyes rolled up to the ceiling and then back to her. "Whatever. I'll deal with them *if* they come knocking. I have no intention of answering your questions, no matter how hard you try, Miss Morgan. I learned a long time ago not to trust PIs."

"At the fear of repeating myself, that's a shame, Mr Rattner, not all PIs are cast in the same mould, just like coppers aren't. For your information, my fiancé is a local copper. He doesn't appear to have a problem with my role in the community, so I can't understand why a total stranger should give two hoots about the career path I've chosen to take."

He mumbled something incoherent. She thought about asking him to repeat it but decided against it. She was aware deep down there was the odd battle in this life that wasn't open to being won. This was obviously one of those occasions.

"I need to get back to Belinda. She'll be reliant on my compassion over the coming days and weeks." He turned to walk away from her.

"It's a pity she didn't consider you compassionate when she was married to you, otherwise you wouldn't have gone through a needless divorce."

He spun around and glared at her. "Don't judge someone before you know the full facts of what has gone on in their past, Miss Morgan."

"Then tell me. Or else I will continue to make assumptions as to why you're intent on blocking me."

"I'll speak to the police, if the necessity arises. What happened to our marriage is something neither of us wishes to discuss. You'd be advised not to go behind my back and ask her either."

"Advised or *warned*, Mr Rattner? Because from where I'm standing, you appear to be threatening me, not only with your words but also in your stance as well. Surely, even an ex-copper with your experience can see how you're coming across to a total stranger. If I were the suspicious type, I'd be digging deep into your past, trying to establish why you appear to be so angry when I've barely spoken two words to you. Okay, before you accuse me of exaggerating, I admit the 'two words' of my statement could be deemed a stretch of my imagination."

"You don't let up, do you?"

Ruth smiled. "No, I'm a British bulldog through and through. Tenacity and determination could be deemed to some as bad traits of mine. They're the prime reasons I've achieved the results I have in the past and why I intend to stick with being a private investigator in the future."

"You appear to be cocksure of yourself, too. One day, in the not too distant future, I hope someone swipes that smug look off your face, Miss Morgan. You know what? I think you're right. You have probably chosen the correct career, judging by the character traits you've displayed today." He turned again and left the room.

Ruth's heart pounded, and her mouth gaped open for several minutes after he left, until another bout of determination helped her recover from the confrontation and jolted her into joining the others in the lounge.

"I'd better be going now, Cynthia. It was a fleeting visit to bring you up to date. I'll be contacting the inspector this afternoon to appraise her of what I've learned so far from the people I have spoken to." Her gaze drifted over to Rattner.

His eyes narrowed in a warning glare.

Ruth smiled at him, and Cynthia walked her to the front door. "Just checking, Gerald is definitely not staying with you, is he?"

"Nope, he'll be staying at the hotel with the others. Thank goodness the hotel had the rooms available to take them. Not sure how we would have coped otherwise."

"Good for you. It's not as if Belinda is family, is it?"

"That's what I told Reg after hearing your advice earlier. He agreed. He's had enough of walking on eggshells and wants his house back as much as I do."

"He needs to grieve, you both do. It has been a shock for all of you, not just Belinda." She hugged Cynthia and left the house. "I'll be in touch soon, hopefully with some good news. Take care."

"Good luck."

Ruth made a fuss of Ben when she returned to the courtesy car. It was getting late, past five now, and she should be getting home. The trouble was, she was suddenly filled with dread knowing that she would be going home to an empty house. Why was it that most of the time people craved having their own space now and again, however when it was forced upon them, they found it hard to handle?

As it was already dark, she decided to go home and take Ben for a long walk around the block. She passed her sister's house on the way back. Ian, Carolyn's son, was closing the curtains to the lounge. He knocked on the window and waved at her, peered over his shoulder, spoke to someone behind him and then gestured for her to come in.

She raised her thumb and gave Ben's collar a gentle tug. "Come on, boy, want to play with Ian and Robin?"

Ben whimpered, and his tail wagged, which was all the response she needed.

Ian opened the door and bent down to hug Ben. He removed his leash and patted his thigh. "Come on, Ben, come play with me."

Ruth watched them run through the house.

"Hello, you. Everything all right? You seemed miles away," Carolyn asked, stepping into the hall to take Ruth's coat.

"I'm fine. It's been a long day. Make that a long couple of days since we last met."

"Want to talk about it over dinner?"

"Are you sure I'm not putting you out?"

"Nonsense, it's spag bol. Do you want to give James a ring, see if he wants to join us?"

Unexpected tears filled her eyes. "There wouldn't be any point in that, he's staying with a friend for a few days."

They were en route to the kitchen. Carolyn stopped dead in the middle of the hallway and spun around to face her. "What? Why? Oh, love, you two haven't fallen out, have you?"

Ruth nodded. "Yep. The day after my damn birthday. Can you believe it?"

"I'll make a coffee, and you can tell me all about it."

"Not for me. I've not long had one at my client's house. Can I help with dinner?"

"You could lay the table for me."

"Deal."

Halfway through laying the table and with the spaghetti now boiling in the pan, Carolyn stood beside her. "Why do I get the sense you're avoiding me?"

"I'm not. I don't think it's right to burden you with this, that's all."

Carolyn placed her hands on top of Ruth's, preventing her from laying the final setting. "You're not. I'm asking if I can help. If this had happened a few months ago, I might have been guilty of dodging the question, too much on my plate. Now the renovations are complete, I'm all yours."

Ruth collapsed into one of the chairs. In the distance, she could hear the children calling Ben's name and chasing him around the living room. *Wouldn't it be lovely if my life was less complicated?* "You don't want to be saddled with all my problems. We're taking a break from each other for a few days."

"But why? You seemed to be the perfect couple on Saturday. What on earth could have happened to have altered that within twenty-four hours?"

"Things."

Carolyn groaned. "If you don't want to talk about it then that's your prerogative."

"Great, now you're going to fall out with me as well. Just what I need."

"Don't be daft. I'm offering you my shoulder to cry on. It's up to you if you want to decline the offer. I hate seeing you so upset. I know how much you love James. Crikey...has he been cheating on you? Is that it?"

"No. It's not that. At least, I don't think it is. All right, you asked... Prepare for me to have a meltdown, though."

Carolyn glanced over at the stove.

"See, you're too busy, and all I'm doing is taking up your family time."

"Nonsense. I'm all ears. I've still got to keep an eye on dinner." She rose from the table to stir the two pots. "Can you give me the brief version before the rest of them descend on us?"

"Okay, I think getting engaged was the worst mistake I've made in decades. Is that succinct enough for you?"

"What? Now you're just being ridiculous. You and James were made for each other. Your problem is that you've always been a commitment-phobe, and now that you've succumbed and he's slipped a ring on your finger, you're too busy searching for the negatives in your relationship."

"What utter nonsense that is. Hey, may I remind you that I'm not the one who walked out? He is."

"You must have pushed him, hard, if he's packed his bags. Couples who fall out rarely go to that extreme unless they've been pushed too far."

"I didn't, I swear. This was all to do with the investigation. You know what? It's all a blur to me. Everything happened so fast I can't even tell you how it all came about."

Carolyn gave her one of her I-know-you're-trying-to-pull-the-wool-over-my-eyes looks. "Don't give me that. Spill?"

"All right, don't nag. We fell out over that inspector. Here's the bizarre thing: she and I met up at my client's house and agreed to share information on the case."

"Is James aware of that?"

"No. I haven't contacted him. You know how stubborn I am. If I back down now, then he's won."

"For goodness' sake, Ruth, you're sitting at my table, your eyes welling up with tears every time you mention the man's name. What does that tell you?"

"That I'm distraught."

"Get a grip, girl. You love him, we all know that. You're the one who seems to need reminding of the fact now and again. One of these days, that man isn't going to want to stick around if you keep falling out with him over the simplest of things."

"Whoa! Now wait just a second. It was his choice to leave, not mine. Why am I getting the blame here?"

"You're not. All I'm saying is, why don't you take a step back now and again? See your relationship from his perspective. You're both guilty of being pig-headed. It's how you overcome whatever will define your future as a couple that's important."

Ruth contemplated Carolyn's words for a moment. Her sister was right. "Thanks."

"For what? Making you see sense?"

"If that's how you want to phrase it, then yes. I'll try and ring him later."

Carolyn shot her another one of her looks.

"All right, I'll bite the bullet and call. See if we can get a conversation started."

"A few choice words should feature in that conversation, too, like 'I'm sorry'."

"For what? I didn't do anything."

"Whether you did or didn't say anything out of order, it's up to you to compromise. Marriage is all about compromise at the end of the day."

"There's a simple answer to that one, I'm not married."

"As near as. Which reminds me, have you set a date for the wedding yet?"

"Your timing to ask that, sis, is unbelievable," Ruth replied, shaking her head.

"Weddings and the lead up to them are always fraught. Both of you need to take that into consideration when you finally sit down and discuss what is going on between you."

"We haven't even started the planning stages yet. Now can you see why I postponed getting engaged for ten years?"

"If you don't want a large wedding and all that it entails, then you should run off and elope. You're living together anyway—well, sometimes you are when you're not busy sniping and falling out with each other."

Ruth knew her sister was right. The harshness of her words were getting to her, though. She bit down hard on her tongue in case she was put in another unenviable position and managed to fall out with Carolyn as well. "Okay, you've managed to slap my wrists enough now. Is dinner ready yet?"

"Not far off. Would you mind rounding up the troops?"

"Where's Keith?"

"Down the bottom of the garden in his new man-shed. Oh, I forgot, you haven't seen it yet. Go and see for yourself, it's humongous, takes up at least a third of the garden. I'll see to the boys. Will Ben have some sauce?"

"I'd rather not. It's a bit rich for his stomach. It has onions in it, doesn't it?"

Carolyn nodded and seemed puzzled by the question.

"They're toxic to dogs, didn't you know that?"

Carolyn appeared horrified by the startling revelation. "Good job we haven't got a dog. I probably would have killed it years ago. I use a lot of onions in my meals, and the kids invariably have leftovers which I usually chuck in the bin. It would have been a different story if I'd had a dog around."

Ruth shuddered at the thought. "We live and learn. I'll be right back."

She trotted up the back garden to the man cave. Her sister wasn't wrong when she said it was humongous. She called out his name, not wishing to scare him by poking her head in unannounced.

"I'm in here, Ruth. Come in. I don't bite."

The array of tools and the tidiness of the shed took her breath away. "Crikey, I don't think I've ever seen a shed in this condition before. Go you. How's your hand? I hope you're not overdoing it?"

"No, there's no chance of me doing that, not if I want to remain in Carolyn's good books. Everything okay with you? You seem a little down, haven't got your usual sparkle about you."

"I'm fine. A slight domestic problem that I'll not bore you with. Anyway, I'm acting as a messenger. Carolyn is about to dish up, and she asked me to come and fetch you. Do you need a hand clearing anything up?"

"Nope, I was only pottering, so I'm good to go. Are you staying for dinner?"

"Yes, I wasn't intending to, but she twisted my arm. Is that all right with you?"

He tutted. "Don't be so insulting, of course it is."

Outside the shed, he threw an arm around her shoulder, and they walked back to the house together. Ben was standing at the back door, looking for her. She bent down and pecked him on the head. "Having fun, boy?"

He whimpered, wagged his tail and went in search of the boys once more.

The meal was stunning, as usual. Carolyn was an exceptional cook. Ruth had her moments, but most of the time the responsibility of cooking fell on James' shoulders because generally he was home earlier than her. She refused the offer of ice cream for pudding, helped Carolyn wash and dry up and then left around seven-thirty.

Ruth let Ben in the house ahead of her. The sound of the TV on in the distance made her rush into the lounge and curse herself for having left it on that morning. She found James sitting on the sofa and making a fuss of Ben.

"Hey, you. You've put in a long day," he said.

"What are you doing here? You near as dammit gave me a heart attack."

His smile slipped, and his tone altered. "Charming, it's lovely to see you as well."

"Sorry. Why didn't you ring, let me know that you were coming back?"

"I wasn't aware that I needed your permission to come home. Are you expecting someone for dinner? Is that why you're snapping at me?"

She sighed heavily. "Don't do this, James. Don't turn the tables on me, make out all of this is my fault, and don't, please, don't ever accuse me of seeing someone else behind your back."

"Wow! Steady on there. Who accused you of seeing someone else?"

"You did, in a roundabout way."

It was his turn to let out an exasperated sigh. "I cooked dinner. It's up to you if you want to eat it or not."

She cringed. "I've already eaten. Not what you think either. I stopped off at Carolyn's, and she took pity on me, forced a spag bol down my neck."

"Why are you persisting with this, Ruth?"

"With what?" She was genuinely surprised by his question.

"It seems to me as though you're intent on pushing me away."

She widened her eyes in surprise. "How do you make that out? Because someone was kind enough to take pity on me and feed me, you see that as pushing you away? May I remind you that you walked out on me and you haven't had the balls to contact me since then? How am I to blame for any of this?" Her heated blood seared her veins.

He thrust himself out of the chair. Ben sat on the sofa, his ears pinned back, staring at them warily.

"You're scaring the dog," Ruth said, struggling to find anything else to say.

"And there we have it, it's all about *him*, isn't it?"

"Don't blame Ben. He's got nothing to do with this. What's wrong with you? If you want to end our relationship then tell me, James. I won't be treated this way. Not by you or anyone else come to that."

"You really are a piece of work, Ruth. One small tiff, and you're treating me as though I'm a serial killer. If you want to end it, just say the word, and I'll pack my bags and move out. No, don't bother, I think I've got the hint by now. Why I've wasted ten years on you..."

Ruth crossed her arms. "Go on, say it. Don't hold back, not on my behalf."

"You're not worth the hassle. I thought I loved you; however, in the last few months, since we announced our engagement, you've changed, and not for the better, I hasten to add."

She unfolded her arms and jabbed a pointed finger in his chest. "I've changed? I think you're delusional."

"Really? Well, if that's how you think, then there's no point in me sticking around, is there?"

"No, I suppose you're right about that." She held out her hand. "I'll have the key, if you don't mind. That way you can't come and go as you please."

He dropped it into her hand. "As if that was likely."

She shrugged. "And you're here this evening because?"

"If you must know..." He flung an arm out, and it dropped to hit his thigh. "Why am I bothering? It's obvious you want me out. My guess is you've been angling for it for a while, am I right?"

"As I said, you're delusional if you think that. You're full of anger, even an idiot can see that. I think it'd be best if you leave now and call back for your stuff another time."

"With pleasure. A word of advice for you, Ruth."

She tilted her head and crossed her arms again.

"Take stock of your life before it spirals out of control. You're not getting any younger, you know."

"What's *that* supposed to mean? That I'm going to have a struggle getting another date? Maybe I've had it with men. Most of you only want to change us women anyway, turn us into your mothers. To clean and cook for you..." She paused, aware that she'd gone too far and none of what she'd just said could be aimed at James who had always bent over backwards to do anything that was needed to be done around the house while she got her detective agency up and running.

He glared at her. "Said something you shouldn't have, Ruth? That makes a change, doesn't it? Over the years I've bitten my tongue more times than I care to remember when you've sat on that sofa, slating my boss. The trouble with you is that no one is allowed to think for themselves, are they? It's your way or the highway. Well, this guy has had enough of playing second fiddle not only to that damned career of yours but to Ben as well." He stormed out of the room.

The first thing she did was pat Ben on the head and tell him everything would be all right. Then she chased after James. He was in the kitchen, tearing a plate of food out of the oven.

"You won't be needing this, I'll take it. It was supposed to be an olive branch. Cooking for you has always been a pleasure. Well, not any more. You're on your own now, Ruth. Have a good life." He picked up his black holdall and marched out of the back door, slamming it behind him.

Ruth sank to her knees, buried her head in her hands and rocked back and forth. How had things escalated so quickly? Was she to blame or was James?

Ben appeared beside her, sat, offered his paw and licked her face.

"It looks like it's you and me from now on, boy. You and me…"

7

*T*he insistent ringing of the phone woke Ruth the following day at two minutes to six. She threw back the covers, momentarily disorientated by the noise, and answered it. "Hello? This better be good at this time of the morning."

"Oh gosh, what time is it?"

Recognising her friend's voice, she asked, "Gemma, is that you?"

"It is. Ruth, I'm so sorry to wake you at this ungodly hour, I didn't know who else to turn to."

"Calm down, take a breath and tell me what's going on."

"It's Wayne. I've been informed he's in hospital. Oh God, I don't know what to do for the best. I should get down there but I'm too scared to go."

"Whoa! Back up a second here, Wayne? Isn't he your ex?"

"Yes. We stopped seeing each other a few years ago, but I always tell my exes to contact me if ever they need my help. You know me, I'm not the type to turn my back on people just because they fall out with me."

"You're amazing, a far better person than I am," she replied as memories of the evening before oozed into her fuzzy mind.

"Nonsense. If you heard an ex was in trouble, you'd do the same, I'm sure you would."

"We'll agree to differ on that one. What's wrong with this Wayne anyway?"

"I'm not sure. The hospital rang, said he was asking for me and could I come and see him."

"They must have given you more than that, love."

"I swear, Ruth, they didn't. I was wondering if you'd come to the hospital with me—if you've got nothing else on, that is... I'm so stupid, I know how busy your life is."

"Well, I am in the middle of an investigation..."

"Oh, okay, sorry I called you..."

"If you'll let me finish, I was going to say I can probably spare you a few hours this morning. When were you intending to visit him?"

"Within the next hour. Do you want me to pick you up?"

"No. I'll meet you there, then I can continue with my day once we've finished."

"Can you make it within thirty minutes?"

"I should think so, now that I've managed to come around. Please, in the future, can you leave it until gone eight to ring me? A girl needs her beauty sleep. It's not cool to be interrupted halfway through the night."

"Get you. It's six o'clock, Ruth, that is *not* halfway through the night."

"Maybe in your world, but in mine it definitely is. I'll see you there soon." She ended the call and swept back the quilt, covering Ben in the process. He moaned and rolled over, his legs pushing the quilt up high above his head. She laughed, sought out his nose and kissed the tip. "Time to get up, lazybones. I'll have a quick shower before I let you out."

He didn't move a muscle and drifted back to sleep.

Ten minutes later, Ruth was showered and dressed in a pair of smart jeans and a thick woolly jumper. There was a definite chill in the air already, the type you always tended to associate with living in a house as old as the one she resided in, which lacked enough insulation.

Anyway, she'd much rather have a home rammed to the rafters with character than one of those new builds they insisted on erecting on every available plot these days. She pulled her long red hair back into the usual ponytail, aware she was likely to catch a cold going out with it wet, but also aware she didn't have time to blow-dry it either.

After tending to Ben's needs, she secured him in the back of the courtesy car and headed for the hospital. An excited Gemma waved from her position on the steps by the entrance to the hospital as Ruth pulled into the car park.

"Hopefully, I won't be long, boy. Then I promise you can chase the squirrels for half an hour or more."

Ben licked the side of her face. She was lucky to have him. The only man in her life who didn't give her grief. A stark reality, but the truth, nonetheless.

Gemma hugged her tightly. "Let's get inside quickly, your hair is still wet."

"Don't fuss, it's fine. Where is he?" she asked, distractedly searching the board for which coloured line to follow.

"It's not up there. Well, it is...what I mean is, there's no colour line, I've already checked. We have to go up three floors to the men's ward."

Ruth hooked her arm through Gemma's. Her friend was on the chubby side, her clothes always too tight. Today she had on a floaty dress which stopped halfway up her thigh. Thankfully, underneath she had on a pair of tight leggings that clung to her manly calves. Ruth had always admired the way her friend rebelled against the latest fashion trends, a bit like herself, only she was a tad more conservative in the 'normal clothes' she chose to wear.

Gemma had a heart of gold, and she was wearing her heart on her sleeve at the moment. Ruth was hoping it didn't get hurt in the process of finding out why Wayne was currently lying in a hospital bed and why they were on their way to see him.

"Take it easy when we get in there. If I were in your shoes, I'd be reining in my emotions, keeping a firm hold on them. Prepare for some kind of sob story."

"You think? Oh my, well, I suppose he always was a tinker in that department."

Ruth halted. "What? As in, he has always told you a sob story or that he's some kind of a liar?"

Gemma nodded, her smile slipping from her ruddy features.

"Good Lord, and you've dragged me out of bed to be here, to visit someone whose character is flipping questionable?"

"I'm sorry, Ruth. I feel so ashamed to get you here under false pretences like this. Please don't be mad at me."

She shook her head, disappointment filling every vein in her body. "You're unbelievable. He'd better have a good reason to be here, or I'm likely to add to his damn injuries."

Gemma gasped. "You wouldn't. Oh, heck, don't make me regret calling you. Please, hear him out first before you jump down either of our throats." Gemma took a step towards her, hooked her arm through Ruth's and propelled her forward, in spite of her reluctance.

Dread circulated through Ruth's unenthusiastic body. *Why do I always get drawn into things that don't concern me? Why?*

They entered the lift, and even though Gemma hummed a merry tune to herself, the atmosphere remained decidedly frosty.

Gemma grabbed Ruth's arm again and steered her hesitant frame out of the lift and along the corridor to the men's ward. They applied the antibacterial gel and entered through the swing doors. The nurse's station was immediately in front of them. However, judging by the way Gemma was frantically wriggling and waving beside her, she guessed her friend had already located her ex.

"We're here to see Wayne. Um, Gemma, will you behave for a moment? What's his surname?"

"Bright. Wayne Bright."

Ruth rolled her eyes up to the ceiling. *Bright by name, dumb by nature by the sounds of things*, she thought, harshly. "Wayne Bright. Is it okay if we see him this early? We promise to be quiet."

"We don't usually allow visitors at this time of the day; but, I'm willing to make an exception in this case. The doctor is due to see Mr Bright at nine this morning."

"We'll make it quick, you have my word."

"It looks like your friend has already spotted him. Try and keep the noise to a minimum, there are still patients trying to sleep on the ward."

"We will." Ruth tugged on Gemma's arm. "Did you hear what the Sister said?"

"I did. I'll be quiet, I promise. I just need to see him, make sure he's okay and find out why he's in here."

The nurse nodded, a knowing glint in her hazel-coloured eyes.

Gemma led the way to the bottom of the ward. Wayne was propped up against his pillows. He turned to glance out of the window as they got closer to his bed.

"Hello, love. How are you feeling?" Gemma asked, placing a hand over his and leaning in for a kiss.

He faced them but managed to dodge Gemma's lips by an inch or so. "Don't touch me, I hurt all over." Not a hint of a smile of appreciation coming from him.

Ruth could tell what type of man he was from the outset, without needing to use any of her detective skills. A man who wanted everything and was willing to give nothing in return, a selfish streak running through his core.

"This is my dear friend, Ruth."

He grunted and gave a brief nod in her direction, their gazes never meeting.

Ruth's suspicion radar was on full alert. Yes, the man was black and blue and undoubtedly in severe pain, yet there was something about his demeanour that rankled her. Ruth decided to stay quiet unless either Gemma or Wayne asked for her opinion.

"Bloomin' heck, Wayne, what happened to you? Pick a fight with a giant or something, did you?" It sounded to Ruth like Gemma was trying her best to keep her emotions in check, keeping her tone light and breezy.

Wayne's eyes narrowed. "You think this is some kind of joke?"

"No, not at all. It's my way of dealing with the stress, that's all."

"Christ, yep, I remember now how insensitive and moronic you can be at times. I called you for help, and you come here cracking mindless jokes."

Ruth had to bite down on the vicious retort clinging on to the edge of her tongue. *How dare he speak to her like that? What an absolute jerk.*

Tears filled Gemma's eyes, and the odd one tumbled down her flushed cheeks.

He threw an arm up in the air and winced as it dropped back onto the bed beside him. "Please, give me a break, not the damn waterworks."

Ruth was seething inside. If he continued the way he was going, there was no way she'd be able to remain quiet for long.

"I'm sorry," Gemma murmured.

"You always were after the event. I see you haven't learnt how to engage your brain first before opening that trap of yours," Wayne complained.

His tone was vicious and cruel, reminding her of how James had recently spoken to her. *Are they from the same mould? Maybe that's why I have held off marrying him all these years.*

Gemma gasped again, and more tears fell.

Ruth suggested, "Why don't you get us a drink, Gemma? I could do with a coffee."

"Makes sense to me, for you to make yourself useful instead of standing there crying," Wayne barked at her.

Gemma left the ward. Ruth took a few steps closer until her legs were touching the side of the bed. She rested her hands on the blanket. Wayne's gaze dropped and then shot back up and hooked on to hers.

"Right, buster, while she's out of the way, you and I are going to have a little chat."

"Oh, we are, are we?" he sneered.

Ruth located a bruise on his arm and latched on to it with her fingers. "Yes, we are. Stop with the crappy attitude. Gemma has gone out of her way to come and see you today, and you've done nothing but take a swipe at her since we got here."

He yelled out in pain until Ruth released her hold on him. "I don't know who the hell you are, lady, but let's get one thing straight: I never asked you to come here."

"I know, *she* did. Gemma wanted my expert opinion. You might not know me; however, I'm well-known in this community for being a no-nonsense private investigator. I'm suspecting that's why Gemma asked me to accompany her here today. She was probably under the impression that you might be in need of my help. Let me tell you something, buster. That help just went out of the window. No one treats my friends the way you have in the last five minutes and gets away with it. To me, you've been beaten up. My guess is that you asked for that beating because of your vile temper and the vicious tongue in your head. Am I right?"

"No."

"No, you weren't beaten up?"

"No, I mean yes. I was beaten up, through no fault of my own, though."

Gemma returned carrying two cups of coffee. She handed one to Ruth. "Has he told you what happened yet?"

"Wayne and I have been getting on like the proverbial house on fire. He was just about to open up and tell me who put him in hospital, weren't you?"

"I was?"

Ruth nodded and smiled. "You were. By the time it takes for us to finish our drinks, how's that? I know you're reluctant to tell us who wiped the floor with you. In my experience, it's best to dig deep and search for the courage, even if you were at fault."

"I was *not* at fault. Well, maybe a little. Your friend here can be mighty persuasive, Gem."

"I can. You were saying?" Ruth jumped in.

"It was a loan shark," Wayne replied, all the fight gone from his tone.

Ruth was unsure how to feel about the man now. Whether to berate him for being stupid enough to go down the loan shark route or to feel sorry for him for not being able to meet the imposed payments on any agreement he'd put his signature to.

"Oh, no, that's terrible. How much do you owe?" Gemma asked tentatively, as if expecting him to tear into her again.

"Five grand. Don't judge me. I lost my job last year and fell on tough times. I had to take out a loan in order to survive."

"Five thousand?" Gemma asked, horrified.

"It's not that much, Gem. Some of my friends are in far worse debt than that."

"Who told you to go to the loan shark?" Ruth demanded.

"My friends told me to get involved with him. I signed the contract without reading the small print."

Ruth tutted and shook her head. "Good friends you've got yourself there. Go on, surprise me, what was this loan shark's interest rate?"

His gaze drifted down to the bed again, and he clenched his fists on either side of him. "Something like a thousand percent. Before you have a go at me and tell me how foolish I've been, I know. I tried to bargain with the man, and this was the result. It's going to take me an eternity to pay him back."

"That's the thing when you get into bed with a bunch of sharks, you'll be drowning in deep water for years," Ruth replied, her exasperation evident.

Wayne laid there silent for a while.

It suddenly dawned on her why he'd rung Gemma. "Why have you contacted Gemma after all this time?"

Wayne glared at Ruth for daring to ask the obvious question. He reached out a hand to Gemma, and she slipped hers into his. "Because she has always cared about me. Even when we broke up, she's stayed in touch all these years. She's a caring person, one of the best this world has to offer."

"Aww...I do my best. I've always thought the world of you, Wayne," Gemma purred, oblivious to his game.

"Ah, but it's her gullibility that draws you to her, isn't it?" Ruth refused to hold back a moment longer.

"Ruth! How dare you say that?" Gemma reprimanded, lowering her voice so that other patients couldn't hear her.

"Think about it, Gemma. He's after your money to get him out of the fix he's in."

"He wouldn't do that to me, would you, Wayne?"

"Of course I wouldn't. Don't listen to her, love."

Ruth tilted her head and stared at each of them in turn. She let out a frustrated breath, flung her hand in the air and said, "Whatever. I'm out of here, guys. I have better things to do than see this man twist you around his little finger in the hope that you'll buckle and transfer some money into his account to pay off his debts. See you around, Gemma. A word of caution: heed my warning, otherwise, don't come running to me when it all goes tits up."

"Tell her she's wrong, Wayne, you wouldn't do that to me, would you?" Gemma said as she strode away. Ruth continued walking, not wishing to hear what Wayne's reply was. She marched down the stairs to the entrance, her blood heating her veins the more she recounted the conversation she'd just been privy to.

Gemma was a soft-hearted person who often dwelt in the past. The fact that Wayne dumped her a few years before seemed a trivial matter in her friend's eyes. He had been the love of her life once, that much was evident the second Gemma had laid eyes on him. Ruth had to feel sorry for Gemma—she had an inkling that despite her warning, Gemma was going to be several thousand pounds poorer in the next few days.

Back at the vehicle, she made a fuss of Ben and then walked him around the car park, hoping it would ease her anger. Her mobile rang as she reached the car again. She placed Ben in the back seat and answered the call.

"Miss Morgan, it's DI Littlejohn."

"Oh, hello, Inspector. What can I do for you?"

"Actually, this is about what I can do for you. I have the PM report sitting in front of me. Do you want to drop by the station or would you rather I told you over the phone?"

"Either, I'm not fussed."

"Over the phone it is then, I'm sure we're both up to our necks in work." Ruth heard pages being flipped on the other end of the line, and

Littlejohn let out a sigh. "Ah, yes. Not to put too fine a point on it…the pathologist's conclusion is that Mr Callum Carter was probably murdered."

Ruth fell back against the car and gasped. "No! Really?"

"I'm not in the habit of making up information of this nature during a case, Miss Morgan."

"Sorry. That slipped out. Are you going to tell Belinda, or does she already know?"

"I think I can manage to fit that into my schedule this afternoon, unless you're passing by this morning? Feel free to share the news and that we've scaled up the investigation. We are now classing this as a probable murder inquiry."

"I can pop over there now and break the news, if that's what you want?"

"Do that. Thank you. Do you have anything for me yet?"

"Sadly not. Oh, wait, I do have something that is niggling me."

"I'm listening, go on."

"I called around there yesterday to see if everyone was all right and was surprised to see Belinda's ex-husband there."

"Surprised? May I ask why?"

"Hmm…I don't know really, it just seemed odd to have him show up like that, I mean, so soon after her husband's death."

"Did she call him? Are they still close friends?"

"Yes, she rang him. According to Cynthia, Belinda called a lot of people, and most of them are descending on the town sometime today. I thought I'd pay them a visit over the course of the day, have a chat with them, or would that be deemed as stepping on your toes?"

"Not from where I'm sitting. We've agreed to put our differences aside and to work together on this case. All I ask is that you keep me informed. Did you have a chat with the ex-husband?"

"I did, sort of."

"Either you did or you didn't, Miss Morgan, which is it?" Littlejohn asked, sighing impatiently. At least that was what it sounded like to Ruth.

"I did. Let's just say he wasn't forthcoming with any information."

"Why? Did he give you a reason why he wasn't prepared to speak to you?"

"He's an ex-copper and suspicious of PIs."

Littlejohn let out a full belly laugh. "I know that feeling. I'm glad we've overcome our differences. Do you want me to contact him? Maybe I can change his mind about talking to you."

"He was pretty adamant that he would never go out of his way to speak with me on this matter, only to the police."

"What's your gut telling you? Could he be behind Carter's possible murder?"

"Gosh, I'd hate to cast aspersions against someone just because they refuse to deal with me; however, I have to say that my instincts are telling me there is something awry. It might be worth you sending one of your team out to question him, see if he'll open up to them."

"I'll do that. I'm sure he's got nothing to do with the incident, he's simply dead against PIs. Like me."

"Some of us do an outstanding job, though, you have to agree," Ruth replied, not prepared to let her get away with sniping at her.

"Now and again, I have to admit that's true. Anything else for me?"

"No, that's it for now."

"Right, I'll be off then. Oh, before I go, I wanted to offer my commiserations to you."

"For what?" she asked, perplexed.

"The breakup of your engagement. James was down this morning. I pulled him into the office and ordered him to tell me what is going on. I'm sorry. You two made a good couple."

Ruth found herself dumbstruck for a second or two. She stared down at the engagement ring adorning her finger. "Thanks. All good things come to an end sooner or later, I guess," was all she could muster up as a response before she ended the call.

Flopping into the driver's seat, stunned that it really was over between them and that she no longer had a fiancé, she tore off her engagement ring. She opened the glove box and threw it inside. The anger she'd tried hard to disperse moments earlier was on the rise again. She steadied her breathing, taking long, deep breaths and letting each one out slowly. *How could he? Share the news with his work colleagues before actually spelling it out to me?* It was unfathomable to think how quickly their relationship had declined in the past few days. Did she really mean that little to him? After the years they'd spent together? The years of him pleading with her to get engaged and for it all to end like this after only a few months and the simplest of arguments?

She shook her head, dejection bringing on unwanted tears which she fought hard not to spill. In the end, she vented her fury by lashing out at the steering wheel half a dozen times and letting out a few choice words that barely touched her lips until a situation like this came around. *How dare he treat me like a second-class citizen, how dare he!*

8

She was in dire need of caffeine. The morning had taken a nasty turn twice already, and she prayed the ominous third devastating thing to rock her world wasn't about to rear its ugly head soon. The coffee shop in the high street was serving breakfast when she got there. She pondered whether to take the plunge and go for a waist-busting fry-up to chase her woes away or whether succumbing to such temptation would actually add to them instead.

By the time she had queued up and got to the counter, her mind was made up. She'd settle on a bacon sandwich instead.

"What can I get you, love?" Bryce asked, modelling the finest example of stained chef's whites she'd seen in a while.

"A bacon sandwich with lashings of ketchup should be enough to chase the blues away, thanks."

He smiled and tilted his head. "You're far too young to have the worry of the world on your slender shoulders, Ruth. You can bend my ear when it dies down a bit, if that'll help?"

"You're too kind, Bryce. You've got enough on your plate—no pun intended—as it is. I'll be fine once I've stuffed your delicious calorie-laden goodies down my neck."

"The offer stands. I'll get your order now. I'll even throw an extra rasher of bacon in there for you." He winked. "I wouldn't do that for everyone, only my favourite PI."

She smiled, it was hard not to. Bryce had always been a fabulous friend over the years. He and his wife Sonya worked hard and reaped the rewards. They had a small motor cruiser sitting in the harbour where they whiled away their days off, the few they took anyway. He'd often invited her and James to join them on one of their cruises around the bay. No chance of that happening now…now that her love life was in tatters and her engagement was in the toilet.

"Ruth? I said that will be three pounds fifty, love. Are you sure you're okay?"

"Miles away. Sorry." She dug in her purse and handed him the right money, knowing that he'd reduced the price for her. She'd make it up to him by leaving a generous tip on the table when she left.

"Take a seat. I'll bring it over when it's ready."

"Thanks, Bryce, you're a sweetheart."

His cheeks coloured up, and he turned back to the grill to continue cooking while his wife took over serving the rest of the customers when she returned from whatever she'd been up to.

Ruth squeezed into a two-seater table next to the window and glanced up the main street, catching a glimpse of the sea at the end of the road. What she wouldn't give to take off right now with Ben, lose herself in a long walk along either the coastal path or the beach, even though the beach had to be her least favourite place at the moment, for obvious reasons.

"There you go, nice and crispy, just how you like it, if I remember rightly." Bryce placed the plate in front of her as well as a bottle of ketchup.

"It looks and smells amazing. Thanks, Bryce."

"Enjoy. I hope it does the trick and brightens your day. I hate seeing you so down, Ruth."

She touched his arm. "Don't go fretting about me. I'll survive, I always do."

He winked at her. "You're a born trooper, that's what you are. An incredible woman and human being."

"Easy tiger. I wouldn't go that far."

"Oops, don't tell Sonya I said that. The last thing I need is a domestic on my hands on a busy day like today. I love the winter." He glanced around at the heaving café and rubbed his hands.

"I'm delighted to see you so busy. Not much time for getting out and about on that boat of yours, though, is there? Do you even venture out on it during the winter?"

"Rarely, truth be told. Hey, spring is around the corner. Don't forget the offer stands for you and James to join us. All you have to do is drop in and invite yourselves for the day."

"You're too kind. We'll see what the near future holds for all of us, eh?"

"I'll leave you to eat your brekkie then. Nice to see the smile on your face again, angel. Never let the buggers grind you down, that's my motto."

"Wise words. I'll be sure to leave a review on your website, don't worry."

He laughed and walked away. She knew he hadn't been hinting at leaving one, but she'd do it all the same. She liked nothing more than supporting the local businesses in the area and often sat in her office, when times were slow, typing up favourable reviews to help their trade. Everyone knew how pivotal reviews were nowadays for any business to succeed.

She tucked into her sandwich, wiping the ketchup off her greasy chin at regular intervals. After she'd finished, she had to admit that the comfort food had helped brighten her mood considerably. Sod the diet for a day. Although, with James no longer living at the house, it dawned on her that her diet was going to drastically suffer over the coming weeks until she got around to preparing the healthy batch meals she used to make before he'd moved in with her. She finished her coffee, left the tip on the table and waved at Bryce and Sonya on the way out.

Ben was peering through the back window at her, expecting a treat of sorts, the way he always did when she visited the café. She pulled out the serviette, carrying the bacon rind and the half a slice of bacon she'd saved for him and placed it on the seat in front of him. "Wait... okay, you can eat it now."

Then Ruth rang Cynthia.

"Hello?"

"Cynthia, it's Ruth. I have some news. Can I drop by and see you, or is it too early?"

"Not early at all, we're all up, and Belinda's visitors have already started arriving. Come over when you're ready."

Poor Cynthia, she sounded harassed. "I'll be there in ten minutes. Don't bother putting the kettle on for me, I've just stopped off at the café in town for my breakfast."

"Nice to have a treat now and again. We'll see you soon, Ruth."

She placed the phone on the passenger seat, started up the courtesy car and smiled at Ben licking his lips in the rear-view mirror. "Scrummy, eh? Stick with me, boy, I'll share the good things in this life with you. Let's face it, I won't have anyone else to share them with in the near future, will I?"

Ben groaned and stretched out to place a paw on her shoulder. Tears welled up in her eyes. *And they say dogs are stupid and they don't understand. Nothing could be further from the truth with my boy.*

*R*uth arrived at the Old Station House around ten minutes later. There were a number of cars parked in the driveway so she decided to leave her car on the main road. She patted Ben on the head and lowered the windows in the back for him. He stuck his nose out and whimpered as she locked the door. "Go to sleep. I'll try and make this quick, and then we'll go for a long walk, I promise."

He settled down on the back seat, and she crossed the short distance to the front door and rang the bell. Cynthia answered it within seconds. She rolled her eyes and grabbed Ruth's arm, yanking her over the threshold.

"What's going on?" Ruth asked, concerned by her friend's reaction.

"I need your assistance keeping the peace in there. Reg is hopeless at that type of thing. He's no help, sitting in the corner, wishing everyone would leave us alone but not having the courage to tell them. It's going to be down to me, as usual, to look the ogre."

"That's unfair. Let me help you out, I'm used to people calling me names or stabbing me in the back. You shouldn't be subjecting yourself to this. All you're trying to do is assist these people during their grief. Hey, you and Reg are grieving, too. They need to understand that. Plus, you've opened your home to these people. They need to start treating you both with respect. I thought they were going to stay at the hotel?"

"They are, but they've agreed to treat our home as a meet-up point. I didn't have the heart to tell them to get on their bikes."

"I'll do that for you, don't worry. We'll get this sorted."

"You're a treasure, Ruth. A good friend as well as an exceptional person."

Ruth hugged her and led the way into the lounge to find a throng of people standing, shouting and pointing at each other. Ruth looked around her, trying to find something to use to draw the group's attention. There wasn't anything. In the end, she resorted to shouting, "Guys, please, everyone. Can we have a bit of hush around here? I've only just arrived and I've already got a headache brewing. Let's show our hosts some respect and keep the noise to a minimum, if you will."

Six sets of warring eyes turned her way. She felt the imaginary daggers find their spot in the middle of her forehead.

"Ruth is right. You all need to calm down a bit," Belinda announced. "Fighting amongst ourselves isn't going to help anyone."

"Thank you, Belinda. Maybe you wouldn't mind introducing everyone to me," Ruth replied.

Belinda cleared her throat and proceeded with clarity, and a little hesitancy in some cases, thrown in. "You know Gerald, my ex-husband, you've already met."

Ruth nodded but chose not to smile at the man who was glaring at her the same way he had the day before.

Belinda continued with the introductions. "This is Marlene Andrews and her husband, Zach. Marlene was Callum's first wife."

"I see. I'm pleased to meet you." Ruth extended her hand to both of them.

"And you are?" Zach asked, suspicion rife in his voice.

"I'm Ruth Morgan, the local private investigator. Cynthia has hired me to investigate the case."

Zach snorted derisively. "What can a PI do for us that the police can't?" he demanded.

Hello, here we go again. Is this a male trait not to trust PIs? Or is there more to it than that?

"Ruth is exceptional. She has solved two murders in the town already, and yes, the police were involved in the cases, but they screwed them up," Cynthia replied, speaking up for her.

A grunt came from the other corner of the room, the one in which Gerald was standing. Ruth didn't even give him the satisfaction of letting on that she'd heard his blatant bout of displeasure. "Thanks, Cynthia. It's not like me to blow my own trumpet; however, if the need arises, I will. Cynthia is right, my skills have been honed rather well over the years. My personal radar has become expert in pointing out a killer, and that's the truth, whether some people choose to believe it or not."

Another grunt came from Gerald, and again she ignored the man's rudeness.

"Okay, I'm sold," Zach replied. "What have you found out so far?"

"I'll leave that for now if you don't mind. Who's next?" she asked Belinda.

"This is Julian, Callum and Marlene's son."

The man with wispy blond hair and a tanned face smiled and gave her a brief nod. "Pleased to meet you. I wish you well in your exploits to discover what happened to my father."

"Thank you. It's good to meet you. My condolences on the loss of your father."

He nodded again, and his head dipped a little.

Belinda stood beside the final person. A man in his late fifties, his grey hair was messed up, either by the wind or the fact he hadn't bothered to comb it that morning. Ruth was thinking the latter. "And this is William, Callum's brother."

She held out her hand again. He was hesitant in his attempt to return the favour but eventually shook it.

"Pleased to meet you," she smiled to put the man at ease.

"Thanks," William replied, unlatching his hand and moving to the other side of the room to peer out of the bay window.

Ruth glanced around; she felt everyone's gaze on her, except William's. "Forgive the intrusion, I wanted to drop by and let you know as soon as I heard the news."

"What news?" Belinda asked, not giving her a chance to add anything else.

"The pathologist has confirmed that your husband's death is being classed as possible murder."

Belinda gasped, and her legs gave way beneath her. Gerald and Marlene each managed to grab one of her arms to break her fall. They guided Belinda to the couch where she sat, dumbfounded, staring at Ruth.

"I'm sorry if the news has come as a shock to you, Belinda."

"Who would hurt Callum...no, kill him, like that? Why? He's never hurt anyone." The tears soon followed, and a sob broke out.

Cynthia sat in the seat next to her and comforted her. "Knowing Ruth the way I do, her dogged determination will get to the bottom of this, won't it, Ruth?"

"I'm hoping so, Cynthia. Together with the police, we'll find the person responsible for this and bring them to justice. Callum didn't deserve to die, no one does. Now, if you wouldn't mind, I need to have a quiet chat with all of you."

"Why?" Gerald demanded sternly.

"I need to find out if anyone has any idea why someone would want Callum dead."

"Are you insinuating one of us did the deed?" Gerald snapped back.

She shook her head. "No, that wasn't what I was thinking at all. Only that someone might have an inkling if Callum has fallen out with someone recently, a person his wife isn't aware of."

Gerald shrugged and said nothing further. *Stick that where the sun don't shine, mate.*

"I think it's an excellent idea, Ruth. Do you want to see everyone individually?"

"Preferably, yes."

"What about using the dining room?"

"That would be perfect. Does anyone have any objection to chatting with me now?" Ruth enquired, scanning the crowd.

"It's not like we're doing anything else, is it?" Gerald mumbled.

"I've already spoken to Gerald and Belinda, so if the rest of you can decide amongst you who I should question first, we can get this show on the road."

"Are you okay now, Belinda? Only I'd like to get the dining room ready for Ruth," Cynthia bowed her head to look into Belinda's eyes.

"I'll be fine. It was such a shock. You go."

Cynthia and Ruth left the room and slipped into the dining room.

Cynthia closed the door behind them and whispered, "What are you thinking, Ruth? Is Gerald right? Do you think one of them is the guilty party?"

"I truly don't have a clue at this stage, hence the need to question them. I doubt it; however, all of them coming here so soon is more than a little mystifying to me."

"Ah, you mean how they have all managed to get the time off work to make the trip?"

"Exactly. Maybe my line of thinking is way off the mark there, I don't know. Let's not make any judgements just yet, we'll see what they have to say first. Maybe one of them knows something that Belinda isn't aware of."

Cynthia placed a hand against her pale cheek. "Oh my, you think Callum had a secret? One that ultimately led to his death?"

"Try not to overthink things for now, Cynthia. Let's see what my questioning reveals and we'll go from there. Have they all booked into the hotel?"

"I think so. I need to chase that up with them all later. Belinda and Gerald stayed at the hotel last night, in separate rooms as far as I know.

They'd arranged for the others to meet them here this morning. A bit of an inconvenience for Reg and me. Hopefully they won't stay around for too long. Reg says they think they're onto a good thing and are expecting me to feed and water them every few hours. Truth be told, I'm physically and mentally exhausted already, running around after them."

"I'm not surprised after the crazy renovating schedule you and Reg have both endured lately. I'll be as quick as I can, and then, if you like, I'll suggest they all head over to the hotel to give you time to grieve the loss of your friend, how's that?"

"You're such a thoughtful person, Ruth. It sounds like a plan to me. I'll leave you to it. Give me a shout if you'd like a drink. I don't mind playing hostess to you because you're doing a worthwhile job."

"And I'm on the payroll," she replied, winking. "I'm fine, honestly. Take care of yourself and Reg, blow the others, and me, of course."

"We'll see. I might spout off that I hate being taken for granted, but doing something like that goes against the grain with me. There, the room is tidy enough for you, yes?"

"It is, you're the perfect hostess."

Cynthia's cheeks flushed. "Do you need any paper, you know, to note down their answers?"

Ruth withdrew an A5 spiral bound notebook from her bag and set it down on the polished mahogany dining table. "I'm sorted, thanks."

They returned to the lounge to find an atmosphere lingering.

"Who wants to go first?" Ruth asked.

Marlene and Zach glanced at each other. Zach nodded at his wife.

Marlene raised her hand slightly. "I will."

"Good, if you'd like to come this way." Ruth motioned for Marlene to join her in the dining room. Once they were both inside, Ruth closed the door.

"Try not to be worried about this interview, Marlene. I'm on a fishing trip, that's all. What I need to find out is if anyone knew something about Callum's past that was likely to get him into hot water, or killed as the case may be. When did you get divorced?"

"That would have been in two thousand and one, eighteen years ago, this month actually. We waited until Julian was eighteen before we took the decision to part permanently."

"By that, I take it you're saying that the marriage had been on rocky ground for a while, is that correct?" Ruth flipped open her pad and prepared to jot down the answer.

"That's correct. Callum was one of those people you sometimes couldn't stand being in the same room with. Saying that, when he wasn't around, you missed him. Does that even make sense? It doesn't to me. I've struggled with it over the years, I can tell you, especially before Zach came into my life."

"When was that?"

"Three years after Callum and I got divorced. It was a whirlwind romance. He swept me off to Venice after a month and proposed to me in a gondola. It was so romantic, how could I say no?"

"How wonderful," Ruth replied, trying her hardest to sound genuine, even though thoughts of the demise of her relationship flooded her mind. "And when did you get married?"

"Not until nine months later. We've been blissfully married for fourteen years now. He's the true love of my life. Callum and I were far too young to appreciate what it takes for a marriage to work."

"A lot of compromise has to take place, if I'm not mistaken?"

"Exactly. That type of thing seems to be more achievable with age. Although saying that, I think it's always tougher to compromise when children are involved. Julian was nineteen when Zach and I got married—he was away at university, which was a bonus for us and our relationship. It was far smoother with less hassles. Are you married?"

"No. Can't see that happening in the foreseeable future either. I tend to prefer my own company, although I'm devoted to my dog. Most men would have a tough time dealing with that." James' words regarding Ben flowed through her mind.

"That's a shame. Everyone deserves to experience real love at least once in their life."

"I'm afraid I'll end up an old spinster, surrounded by a lot of rescue dogs. I don't care for all this romance stuff really. My work means the world to me, though. My career and Ben are the true loves in my life."

"One day true love will come knocking on your door, and you'll find it hard to resist, I promise you."

"I doubt it. I take it you've remained in contact after the divorce went through?"

"Yes, that's right. Mainly for Julian's sake. It wouldn't be fair on him if we were at each other's throats all the time."

"This is a bit of a personal question, and I understand if you don't wish to answer, but why did you and Callum get divorced?"

Marlene clenched her hands together and rubbed her thumbs. "*Irreconcilable differences* was the term cited on the divorce papers. We simply ran out of words to say to each other. We sat there for hours every evening, unable to strike up a conversation. Even when we did manage it, we invariably ended up arguing. I could no longer live like that. I was very timid back then. I'm a different person now, so was he come the end, so I gather."

Ruth nodded, reflecting on what she'd been told about Callum's way of life with Belinda. She seemed to be the one dominating that marriage, not him. "I'm glad you're happy in your new marriage. What about Julian, did he get on well with his father?"

"Thanks. I don't understand why you would say that. Of course Julian got on well with his father. He was devoted to him. This has all come as a huge shock to my son. He's the reason Zach and I are here. We were determined to give him our support at this sad time."

"Does Julian get on with Belinda?"

"You'll have to ask him that. He's always told me he has. I've never pushed the issue with him, just taken his word on it."

"I'll ask him. When you were married to Callum, can you tell me if he had any vices? Anything that may have led him down the wrong path in life, into the hands of unscrupulous people perhaps?"

"Wow, is that who you believe killed him?"

"I'm just asking the question for now. Trying to gather as many facts and as much evidence as I can at this stage."

She thought for a moment and then shook her head slowly. "I don't believe so. How can anyone know what secrets are held by other people in their lives?"

"That's true. Only when something like this happens we do really start to question a deceased person's behaviour."

Tears welled up in Marlene's eyes. "I'm sorry that he's gone; however, I won't be losing sleep over his departure. If that makes me sound cruel and heartless, then so be it. I wasted twenty years of my life with that man. Travelling the globe because of his job, stationed at military bases around the world. Making friends in these places only to move on within a few months or years. A woman needs more stability in her life. Being married to a man in the services isn't all it's cracked up to be. He was a daredevil—that alone caused more arguments in our house than I care to remember."

"I've heard he was into rock climbing."

"More than that. I think the term is *extreme sports*. Anything dangerous, and he was the first one to raise his hand to take on the assignment. A woman can't live her life on the edge like that, no one can. I'm surprised I lasted as long as I did. When he wasn't deployed somewhere, he appeared to go into his shell when he was with me. That in itself was awfully hard to handle."

"I can imagine. I'm sorry you had to go through that for so many years, Marlene."

"It's in the past, no point dwelling on it now. Do you need to know anything else? Can I ask a question?"

"Nothing else. Of course, go right ahead."

"Why are you questioning us and not the police? I don't wish to appear rude here, but why are you doing the police's job for them?"

"Usually I conduct my business alone. However, this time, I'm working alongside the police. I'm sure they'll get around to interviewing you all soon. Cynthia has employed me to find out what happened to Callum, so that's what I intend to do."

"Won't you be stepping on the investigating officer's toes?"

"No. We've fallen out in the past, but we've called a truce for this case and have agreed to work alongside each other."

"That sounds as though it could muddy the waters in a case."

"No, I have confidence in my abilities. I'll pull back and leave it to the experts if I feel out of my depth during the investigation."

"Thank you for clearing that up. Sorry if I offended you at all."

"You didn't. I have very broad shoulders. If there's nothing further you can add, I'd like to move on to the next person now, if that's okay? I don't want to add to everyone's angst by holding them up any more than is necessary."

Marlene rose from her seat and nodded. "Thank you for respecting our grief, whichever form that takes. Who shall I send in next?"

"Would you mind asking your husband to join me next? Thanks."

Marlene smiled and left the room.

While she waited, Ruth doodled on her pad. She glanced up when the door opened and gestured for Zach to sit opposite her. "Thanks for joining me. I'll make this as brief as possible."

"It's a pleasure. If I can help the investigation, I will. What is it you need to know?"

Ruth noticed how relaxed he seemed so right away discounted him as a suspect, although that appraisal could alter once she began asking her questions. "How well did you know Callum?"

"I've met him a few times over the years. We tolerated each other at those meetings, shall we say."

"Tolerated him, why?"

"Mainly because of the way he treated Marlene. I'm not saying he was the type of man to beat her black and blue, but he still didn't show her the love she deserved. She's a wonderful woman and should have been worshipped from the outset. If he'd done that, then their marriage wouldn't have failed."

"And you wouldn't have met and spent the past fourteen years with her," Ruth replied, tilting her head and smiling.

"You have a valid point there. Maybe I should have been more grateful to him over the years."

"Did you ever fall out as such?"

"Not really. I cornered him one time at a social gathering we were both attending to tell him what a fool he'd been. He actually admitted to me that he agreed and he'd regretted his marriage ending the way it had." He chuckled and lowered his voice to add, "Maybe the grass wasn't greener on the other side, eh?"

"Meaning, him choosing to marry Belinda?"

"Oh yes, he ended up well and truly...henpecked is the term, I believe."

Ruth smiled, neither confirming nor denying the statement. "It's a long shot asking you because you don't seem as close as the others were to Callum, but do you know anything that has gone on in his past that could have come back to haunt him and possibly lead to his death?"

Zach vehemently shook his head, his grey eyes clear from any sign of deceit. "No, I can't say I have."

"Is there anything else you'd like to tell me? Perhaps you've overheard a conversation between your wife and her former husband or possibly one she's held with her son regarding his father?"

He frowned. "You're asking if I've ever spied on my wife?"

"Not spied, no. Look, this case has to lead somewhere. All I'm trying to do is search for a possible link which led to Callum losing his life."

"My answer still remains the same. No, I know of nothing which could be seen as a possible clue which might have led to Callum's death."

"Thank you."

He started to stand.

"One last question, if I may?"

Zach flopped into his chair again. "What's that?"

"Can you tell me what you do for a living?"

"Not that it makes a difference. I'm a coach driver for an old folks' home. I do it on a part-time basis, hence us being able to drop everything and come here today."

"I see, and where are you based?"

"In Swanton."

"Thanks, that'll be all."

"Who do you want to see next?" he asked, tucking the dining chair under the table.

"Can you send in Julian? Thanks for sparing me the time."

"No problem."

He exited the room. Ruth jotted down a few notes of interest. Swanton was the first thing she entered. It was a town only forty-five minutes away. It was possible that either Marlene or Zach could have made it there and back within a couple of hours. Or was she guilty of overthinking things again?

Distracted with her thoughts, she neglected to hear Julian come into the room and take a seat. She glanced up from her notebook to find him staring at her, his pale-blue eyes intense and full of sadness.

"I do apologise, I didn't hear you come in. Thanks for speaking with me today, Julian. I'll make this as brief as I can."

"Get on with it. I don't know why you're here anyway. The police should be doing this, not a two-bit PI from a skanky town like this."

Whoa...you've changed your tune, matey. "As I've already explained, Cynthia has employed me to find out what happened to your father and, on this case, the local inspector and I have agreed to share any information connected to the investigation."

"Why? What can someone like you accomplish that the police can't?"

His abruptness took her breath away for a moment or two. "Let's just say I'm good at what I do. I have a proven record that most of my clients appreciate, otherwise, they wouldn't pay for my services. If you're prepared to give me a chance, I'm sure I'll be able to find out who killed your father. If, on the other hand, you decide not to deal with me, like Gerald, then my job is going to be a darn sight harder."

He frowned and asked, "Why isn't Gerald prepared to speak with you?"

She sighed. "Because I'm a private investigator, and being an ex-copper, his trust isn't what it should be towards people plying my trade."

"I see. If you don't mind me saying, where are the police and what are they doing? My father has lost his life, and only you appear to be investigating the case. How do you think that looks to the rest of my family?"

"I've tried my hardest to allay everyone's fears in that department.

The police are doing their bit. If you'll give me a chance, I'm confident I won't let any of you down."

"Hmm…what have you discovered up to this point?"

"I'd rather keep that information to myself, if you don't mind. If I start letting everyone know what I've learnt, it could muddy the waters and tip off the killer."

He sat back and gaped at her. After taking a moment to recover, he said, "You're telling me that you think there's a killer walking amongst us, his own family?"

"No, not exactly. I do have one other lead that I need to chase up. The reason I've asked to have a word with each of you is to see if you can shed any light on any past problems your father might have had. For example, to your knowledge, has he ever fallen out with anyone?"

"Anyone who would likely turn around and end his life? Wow, what a question that is."

"And your answer would be?"

"No, of course. I can't even believe that you would ask such a question, given that his family are grieving his loss."

"I don't mean it to come across as derogatory in the slightest. It truly is a very simple question, one that the police would be keen to find the answer to if the questioning was left to them, I can assure you."

"Maybe it just sounds odd coming from you. No offence."

What? Are you kidding me? You don't expect me to take offence to that? "None taken," she assured him, going against what she'd thought. "Would you mind thinking over the question for a while? Perhaps your father did a deal with someone he wasn't aware was dodgy and it turned out to be the wrong move, something along those lines."

"No, no, no. My father was ex-army. He was an intelligent man after the life experiences he'd gathered throughout his years. His death has nothing to do with anything that's gone on in his past. If it had, he would have been killed at home in Timbleton, not in a sleepy coastal town like this, wouldn't he?"

Ruth shrugged. "Not necessarily. You'd be surprised the lengths killers will go to in order to accomplish their aims. Killing someone in a different town to where they live would be at the top of their list, I can guarantee that."

"I don't understand, why?"

"Less chance of the clues leading back to the killer. Perhaps it was their intention to cast doubt over the actual death. It wasn't until it was confirmed today by the pathologist that your father's true possible cause of death was known. Before the pathologist's findings, the investigating team have treated it as accidental."

"Is that why the police are refusing to get involved and leaving most of the donkey work to you?"

Ruth paused to reflect that notion for a few seconds. "No, not at all. We, as in the police and I, had to work with the evidence to hand at the time. They've done their bit, just like I have."

"And yet you're the one who has drawn the short straw and is questioning the family and friends."

She shrugged again. "I'd rather do that than spend most of my time in my office, going over the few clues that have presented themselves thus far."

"Fair point. So, who is at the top of your list right now?"

"I'm not at liberty to say, Mr Carter."

"*Won't* say or *can't*? As in, we're all leading you a merry dance?"

"I have my suspicions, let's just leave it there, shall we?" she replied elusively.

"What else do you want to know?"

She flipped over to a new page in her notebook and poised her pen. "What is it you do for a living, Mr Carter?"

"It's Julian. I run my own business."

"Doing what?"

"I own a microbrewery. I specialise in cask ales with a deep flavour."

"Interesting. Is there much call for that these days?"

He laughed, and for the first time during their meeting, his frown eased. "Yes, it's becoming more and more popular. The last year alone my business has grown by forty percent."

"That's excellent news, congratulations to you."

"Thanks. It's hard work. I tend to regularly do a ninety-hour week, but the rewards are definitely coming through now."

"As opposed to what? A year ago?"

"Yes, as I said, the business is flourishing now. I suppose any new venture needs time to find its feet in the market. My reputation is growing daily, along with my bank balance, or should I say the business's bank balance. Either way, I'm thrilled by the results and couldn't ask for more."

"Your father must have been exceptionally proud of you."

He turned to glance out of the window. "Yes and no. He berated me for years, told me to get off my backside and do something useful. He was a tough taskmaster. Maybe that was because of his military background, I don't know, I never really got the chance to sit down and speak to him man to man."

"May I ask why?"

He returned his gaze to her, and tears welled up. "It's harder for kids to be treated as equals by their family members. Yes, they can share in their children's successes, but, well, in Dad's case, he's always held back with the praise. Took pride in tearing down any ideas I had to grow the business."

"That's terrible. How did it make you feel?"

"Honestly? Worthless at times. However, Mum and Zach gave me the strength to continue. Zach's a good bloke. Don't get me wrong, I'm not saying my father wasn't a loving man, it's just that Zach has always been there for me to talk to, whereas my father has never really shown that much interest in either me or my mum. Harsh, but true. Maybe if he had shown some interest she wouldn't have divorced him. Saying that, she's far happier with Zach, and he gives her everything she needs."

"When I spoke to him earlier, he seemed a decent enough chap. It takes a lot of guts to take on another man's family."

"It does. He's never wanted children of his own, but that hasn't prevented him from proving how much he loves me over the years."

"I'm glad he's been a constant support to you when you've needed him the most. Does he have a temper?" she asked, thinking back to how annoyed he'd been when they'd first met.

"What an odd question. No, I don't think he's ever raised his voice to me, let alone his hand."

"How well do you get on with Belinda?"

He shrugged. "As well as can be expected, I suppose. She's not what I would call one of life's most genuine people."

"What makes you say that?"

"She changes moods with the breeze. One second she's sharing a joke with you, and the next she can empty a room with her foul mood. Believe me, she's done that several times at family gatherings, I can tell you. People who have travelled miles to share a birthday or anniversary with her, have ended up regretting going out of their way to make her day feel special when she's blown her top."

Ruth noted this down. "Any specific reason why she explodes the way she does?"

"Dad always made fun of her, saying it was the change she was going through."

Ruth glanced up. "The menopause?"

"That's it. I've been around women all my life at work and in my home life, and, well, I've never experienced any form of meltdown in line with what goes on with her. She turns into a she-devil, I swear."

"Has she ever lashed out at anyone during one of her episodes?"

"She's come close to clocking me one on a number of occasions when I was younger, until I got the measure of her and learnt to keep my distance during her meltdowns."

"What about your father? How did he handle them?"

"He handled them, steered clear of her most of the time during her episodes. Between you and me, I got the impression she was faking it."

"Any reason why you would think that, Julian?"

"Because of the gifts Dad gave her the following day after they'd fallen out. I'm not talking the odd box of chocolates here, I'm talking gold bracelets or any other expensive gifts that took her fancy."

"Interesting. Are you telling me these explosive meltdowns were becoming more and more frequent?"

"Maybe. I've never taken much notice of whether that's true or not. I stopped visiting them about a year ago."

"Can I ask why?"

"Couldn't stand Dad's attitude towards my business or the she-devil having one of her moods. Life's too short...damn, did I just say that?" He shook his head, seemingly ashamed.

"You did, you're forgiven," Ruth replied, smiling. "Have you had much to do with Gerald over the years?"

"Not really. He showed up at a wedding of a distant relative of Belinda's last year—that's the first time I'd ever come into contact with him."

"Do you know if he visited your dad and Belinda a lot?"

"You'd have to ask them that. I mean, Belinda and Gerald. I was surprised to see him here. I didn't realise they were that close still. What do you make of their relationship?"

Ruth held her hand up and waved it from side to side. "I'm not sure. He's not one for holding back and has already told me to butt out of the investigation."

"Oops, I said something similar at the beginning of this meeting. I apologise for that."

"It's fine. I've come to expect a certain amount of distrust and animosity from people I interview, until they figure out that I'm not a stereotypical PI."

"I can understand that. Is there anything else I can help you with?"

"I don't think so. Thanks for being open and honest with me. It's surprising how much I've picked up from what you've told me."

"Care to share?"

"People's perceptions of other people's characters can either make or break a case. Thanks for your insight into those around you. My condolences on your father's death."

"Thanks. Do your best to find the person who did this, Miss Morgan."

"You have my assurance I will do my utmost to ensure that happens. Would you send your uncle in now, please?"

"We didn't get around to discussing him."

"Are you telling me you think there's something I should know about him?"

"Not really. Uncle William has always been a bit of a loner. He and Dad were pretty close, though."

"Thanks for the heads-up on that one. It was nice chatting with you, Julian."

"Thanks, you, too. Sorry about my rudeness. Hey, if you're ever in our neck of the woods and would like to go for a drink one day…"

"I'll be sure to check out your microbrewery when the opportunity arises. Is it open to the public?"

"It is. That's a date then…well, you get my drift." The colour rose in his cheeks, and he quickly left the room.

Within seconds, William took his place in the seat opposite her. She introduced herself. The man grunted, his arms crossed defiantly across his chest and his head dipped.

"Thank you for agreeing to speak with me today, William. Is it all right if I call you that, or would you prefer Mr Carter?"

"William is fine. Don't go shortening it to Will or Bill, though, can't stand either of them. Can't understand why people would want to shorten the name their parents gave them."

"Okay, you have my word I won't do that. Were you close to your brother, William?"

"Yes, not so much lately. Not now he's married to that witch. Evil, she is. Looks down her nose at you all the time. I know I'm nothing special and I've been in and out of trouble all my life, but there's no need for her to treat me like she's walked through a field and stood in a cow pat. That ain't right."

"I'm sorry you've had a tough time over the years. Care to elucidate that?"

"I would, if I knew what the word actually meant."

"Sorry. Care to tell me where your life has gone wrong over the years?"

"Not particularly. Why would you want to know that?"

"I'm trying to get a feel for everyone's character, that's all. What sort of trouble are we talking about?"

"Misdemeanours. Nothing too bad. Why do you want to know that?"

"Okay, we're already going around in circles here. All I'm trying to do is find out what happened to your brother. Please, don't feel bad when I ask you general questions."

"General questions? You were doing nothing of the sort. You asked me personal questions that I don't want to answer. Got that?" He raised his head to look at her and sneered.

"I have indeed. I'm sorry if I've upset you, that wasn't my intention."

"You haven't. Well, sort of. Let's move on, not that I can tell you anything."

"When was the last time you saw your brother?"

"Last week. He came over to my house in Timbleton and took me out to lunch."

"That was nice. Was it a special occasion?"

"No. Does it have to be to see your family?" he replied defensively.

"No, not at all. Can I ask why you met up?"

His gaze dropped to the table, and he scratched the left side of his neck. "That's my business and no one else's."

"You're not making this easy, William. All I'm trying to ascertain is what went on in your brother's life leading up to his death."

"Ask away. There's nothing to say I have to answer your damn questions. I'm grieving the loss of my brother. That should tell you enough, lady. Why don't you show us all some respect? Let us get on with mourning the loss of a loved one instead of asking these daft and insensitive questions at this time."

"The others don't seem to have minded that I'm asking these questions."

He snorted loudly. "That's what you think. Everyone out there is of the same opinion: they all think you're butting your nose in where it's not wanted."

"Sorry to hear that. At the end of the day, Mr Carter, all I'm doing is what I've been paid to do. Investigate the possible murder of your brother."

"Do you have to say it like that? Can't you call it 'his death' instead of 'his murder'?"

"Very well, just to appease you. I'm here to investigate the death of your brother. The only way I can do that is by asking you and your family personal questions. It's your prerogative not to answer them."

"Go on, get on with it. If I don't answer you, when the others all have, that'll only make me look guilty in your eyes, won't it?"

She smiled. He wasn't as dumb as he was leading her to believe he was. "Can we start over?"

"Do what you like."

"How was your brother when you met up with him last week?"

"Same as usual. A shadow of his former self since he married that ruddy woman."

"Belinda?"

"Unless he had another wife I didn't know about. Yes, *Belinda.*"

"Did he confide in you?"

He exhaled a large breath. "No, not really. He was one of those military nuts, you know, the type who suppress their true feelings and spend most of their time living a lie."

"Is that what you truly believe?"

"Why shouldn't I? He was a little more relaxed with me when she wasn't around. Even though we met in a café last week, he spent most of the time looking over his shoulder at the door."

"Expecting Belinda to walk in?"

"That's how it seemed to me. Either her or her ex-husband. He's been sniffing around for months, he has. Callum was sick to death of him showing up unannounced at their house, he told me so."

"How long had that been going on?"

"Months, I said, or didn't you hear that?"

Ruth ignored the snarky remark. "Do you know what purpose Gerald's visits had?"

"Nope, you'll have to ask either him or Belinda that. Callum never did open up to me about that."

"Okay, I'll do that. Was Callum happy in his marriage?"

"He told me there were good days and bad days, like every other relationship on this earth, I shouldn't wonder. I've never been involved with anyone, hate the thought of someone telling me what to do and when to do it."

"Did you meet up with Callum regularly?"

"Not that often. I suppose more often than most brothers do at our time of life. Bum, wrong choice of words, given the circumstances. Are we through yet?"

"Soon. Are your parents still alive?"

"No. They both died relatively young—we were both in our thirties. Dad died instantly from a heart attack at home, and Mum died of cancer a few months later. She'd had a lump in her breast for a while, refused to go to the doctor because she knew the prognosis would be bad. She was an idiot; they could have lopped off the breast and she could have survived."

"Yes, she could have had either a lumpectomy or a mastectomy nowadays. I think the options are a lot better than they used to be. Maybe her cancer was too far advanced for the doctors and specialists to save her back then."

"Yep, that's what the doc said all right. She looked terrible on her deathbed. The disease took hold and dragged her down within weeks of her telling us the truth. Now, with Callum gone, well, there's only me left."

"What about Julian, aren't you close to him?"

"Not really. He accepts I'm his uncle, but that's about as far as it goes."

"I'm presuming Belinda rang you to inform you that Callum had died."

"Yep, she did that."

"It must have come as a shock to learn of Callum's death like that."

He shrugged. "Death has always been a part of my life. I miss those who have passed, but life goes on," he said, shrugging again.

"I suppose it comes to us all eventually. There's a difference between a death that is expected, as in, from an illness like your parents suffered, and a death from a murder. It's my job to get to the bottom of this. When you met your brother last week, you said he was constantly looking over his shoulder. Do you truly believe that was because he was expecting Belinda to walk in at any second? Or could he have been agitated about something else altogether?"

His gaze remained lowered, and he shook his head. "I don't know. I guess I assumed he was concerned about Belinda. I didn't have any reason to think otherwise." He ran a hand through his short grey hair. "Why didn't I push him for an answer? Maybe I could have helped him if he'd only opened up to me. Do you think he was in some kind of trouble?"

"Honestly, I don't know the answer to that, and after speaking with the rest of the family, no one has suggested anything of the sort. I'm struggling to find a motive at present. Okay, I think we're done here. I'm sorry for your loss, Mr Carter. I appreciate you taking the time to talk to me."

"Do it for us. Find who did this to Callum. Punish them for taking him from us."

Ruth gathered her notebook and pen, shoved them in her handbag and rose from her chair. "I'm going to try my best."

As William opened the door, the first thing that hit Ruth was the sound of raised male voices. A woman's scream broke out. Ruth barged past William to see what was going on. She found Gerald and Zach in the middle of a full-blown boxing match.

"Stop it! The pair of you," she verbally tore into the men and just about managed to get her slim frame between them.

Belinda and Marlene helped her to prise the men apart.

"What's going on here?" she demanded, her gaze switching between the men.

"He started it," Gerald said, acting like a twelve-year-old.

"No, he started it," Zach replied, sounding equally as childish.

Ruth glanced over at Cynthia and Reg. He had his arm wrapped around his wife's shoulders. They both appeared dumbstruck by what had gone on in their living room.

"Cynthia, are you all right?" Ruth asked, concerned by her friend's colourless cheeks.

Cynthia shook her head. "No. I want them out. All of them. I want my home back."

"Okay, people, you heard what your hostess said. You've overstepped the mark now, all of you. Let's move this somewhere else. Those of you who have just arrived, I believe there have been some rooms set aside at the Carmel Cove Hotel. It's time we let Cynthia and Reg have their home back, allow them to grieve the loss of their dear friend without having to deal with you lot falling out. I'll accompany you to the hotel."

"I ain't got the money to stay in no swish hotel," William complained.

Ruth shot Cynthia a look, warning her not to offer her spare room. Cynthia gave a brief nod of understanding and kept her lips tightly shut.

"Then you'll need to find a park bench somewhere, William," Ruth told him without an ounce of sympathy in her tone.

"Charming, that is. What a town this is. A seaside town where visitors aren't made to feel welcome."

"Don't be so pathetic," Belinda shouted, reprimanding William before Ruth had the chance to do it herself. "I'll pay for your room if necessary."

"I don't care who pays for the rooms, I want everyone out of here in five minutes flat, is that understood? And you two..." She prodded Zach and Gerald in the chest a few times. "You should be ashamed of yourselves, causing unnecessary hassle when people are grieving. In my book, you two shouldn't even be here. The least you can do is damn well behave yourselves rather than add to everyone's grief." It felt good for Ruth slapping Gerald down publicly after the way he'd treated her, refusing to accept her role in the investigation. *Well, take that, tough guy, except you're not that tough any more, judging by the blood coming from your nose.* She silently applauded Zach for bopping Gerald one—she'd been tempted to do just that herself.

The guests tried their hardest to try to persuade Cynthia and Reg to let them stay, but it was Ruth who intervened and ended up shepherding the crowd out of the house. "I'll catch up with you all later.

Belinda has my card. If anyone is thinking of leaving Carmel Cove, ring me before you do. Thank you." She shut the door in their stunned faces.

Going back into the lounge, she hugged Cynthia, who by now had tears streaming down her face. "There, there, let it all out. I'm sorry you had to go through that. They're a bunch of disrespectful people. You and Reg need to spend some quality time together, to grieve without any of that nonsense going on. Selfish, that's what they all are."

"I'll take care of her, Ruth. Thank you for all you've done for us over the past few days, we're truly grateful," Reg said, throwing an arm around his wife's shoulders.

"Nonsense. I'm a friend, it's what friends do for each other. Let me make you both a nice pot of tea, eh?"

Cynthia nodded and slipped into the reclining chair next to the gas fire. Reg smiled and turned the knob on the fire to get more heat into the room. The temperature had dropped considerably now that there were fewer people filling it. Ruth made the couple a pot of tea and hunted the kitchen cupboards for the tin of biscuits. After plating up a selection of shortbread and bourbons, she returned to the lounge, carrying the tray which she set down on the table beside Cynthia.

"Thank you, Ruth, what would we do without you?" Cynthia covered Ruth's hand with her own.

"You'd get by. Okay, I'm going to take my own advice on board and leave you two lovely people alone. No matter what you think right now, you need time to grieve. I'll be on the end of the phone if you need me, remember that. Any more hassle from any one of them, promise me you'll ring me straight away?"

Cynthia placed a hand to her chest, covering the frills on her cream blouse. "Do you think they'll bother us again? As much as I want to help them get over their loss, it was all getting too much for us at this sad time."

"They're guilty of taking you for granted. Maybe not all of them, but you need to get your own lives back on an even keel. You can do without all this disruption. I'll be in touch soon. If any problems crop up in the meantime, call me, okay?"

Cynthia smiled and nodded.

Reg touched her arm and surprised her by pecking her on the cheek. "You're a good person, Ruth. We're lucky to have you on our side."

"I'm the lucky one. I'm going now before the tears start to flow. Take care of each other." She showed herself out of the front door. The rain was coming down in sheets. Pulling her jacket over her head, she ran towards the car.

Ben welcomed her by licking the side of her face. "I'm wet enough, buddy. Let's get back to the office, dry out in front of the fire. Hopefully the rain will die down soon so we can go to the park."

Her words were enough to make him settle down and curl up on the back seat. The office was a short drive away and yet, by the time she drew up outside and parked the car, Ben was snoring gently. He bolted upright to look around when she cut the engine.

"Come on, sleepyhead. Let's see if there have been any calls in our absence." Although she'd switched any office calls over to her mobile, sometimes the system was guilty of failing—not too often, thank goodness.

She entered the office to find no blinking light on the answerphone. After making herself a strong coffee, she settled down at her desk and took out her notebook. The next few hours consisted of her trawling the internet, Googling all the names of the people she'd come into contact with and seeing what she could find out about their back-grounds. If there was information to be had about them, she was tena-cious enough to find it. In her mind, all the people she'd met over the past few days, which included Belinda, had to be considered as suspects. She'd dealt with so many cases in the past, not necessarily murder cases, but cases all the same, where a family member turned out to be the guilty party.

Ruth was getting ready to go home at the end of a long day, her eyes tired from staring at the computer screen all afternoon, when the office phone rang. "Hello, Carmel Cove Detective Agency, how may I help?"

"Glad I caught you."

Inspector Littlejohn's unmistakable voice filled her ear. "I was in the process of packing up. What can I do for you, Inspector?"

"I thought I'd check in with you to see how things were progressing at your end."

"They're travelling in the right direction, I think. I spent a few hours questioning all the family this morning, and this afternoon I've been holed up in my office searching the internet for clues."

"Searching the internet? In what respect?"

"To satisfy my suspicions more than anything."

"Okay, I'm not liking the sound of this. If you have something for us to go on then why haven't you contacted me? What part of 'sharing our information' is it you're having problems with?"

Ruth cringed. By the way Littlejohn's voice had risen, it was clear she'd opened her mouth and said the wrong thing. "I haven't got a problem as such, Inspector. I have already informed you that the family were on their way. You didn't instruct me not to speak to them, neither did you mention that you would prefer to interview them yourself."

"Okay, fair point. Nevertheless, you should have rung me straight away to let me know if any of the interviews had raised your suspicions."

Ruth placed her hand over the receiver and blew out an exasperated breath. *Crap, this is all I need, to end my day with another ten rounds with this one.* "I'm a suspicious type, what can I say? I didn't want to bother you until I had something more concrete to go on."

"I see, and tell me, what has your research uncovered?"

"That my suspicions were spot-on. Each of these people, bar Callum Carter's ex-wife, is causing me to suspect they could be involved in his death."

"Interesting. Do you want to meet up and discuss your findings?"

"What, now?"

"I'm up for an after-work drink at the local, if you are?"

Ruth glanced across the room at Ben, who hadn't had a walk in hours due to the rain. He must be dying for a pee. "Give me fifteen minutes to give my dog a quick walk. Do you know the Four Feathers in town?"

"Of course. I'll meet you there at five-thirty. Don't be late, my time is precious, Miss Morgan."

She had to do it, to take a final swipe. "You have my word." Ruth ended the call and whistled for Ben to join her at the door. Slipping on her coat, she riffled in the basket where she kept a few of his things. She found his coat and put it on. He moaned softly. She was never quite sure if he enjoyed wearing the waterproof material or not. "It'll keep you dry, sweetie. Come on, we'd better get a wriggle on if we aren't going to be late for Her Royal Highness." She switched on the answerphone and locked the office door. Another long day done and dusted. Thoughts of what she could prepare for dinner fleetingly crossed her mind, but that soon passed once she got outside and was forced to concentrate on combating the rain.

On her way to the pub, she stopped off at the village green to let Ben do his business. It was his decision to run for cover after only battling the elements for a few minutes. "Good lad. You have more common sense than most humans I know." She leaned over and retrieved a treat from the glove box.

Ben savoured the bacon rasher treat and settled down on the back seat again. She pulled away and drove the few seconds down the road where she parked in the Four Feathers' car park. "I won't be long. If she starts giving me grief, I'll be back quicker than you can have forty winks." She stroked his head and tickled him under the chin. He barked until she reached the entrance to the pub, the way he always did before she disappeared out of sight.

Scanning the public bar area, she spotted Littlejohn sitting in the corner, a tall glass in her hand. She stopped off and ordered an orange juice from the barman, even though she was tempted to order a vodka and tonic to prepare her for going into battle with her adversary.

Littlejohn gestured for her to take a seat on one of the spare stools around the small table. "Thanks for being prompt. I have somewhere I have to be later."

Ruth was dying to ask what she meant but refused to let the question seep out. Instead, she took her notebook from her coat pocket and placed it on the table next to her. Taking a sip of juice to moisten her mouth, she began telling Littlejohn what she knew.

"Wait, before you go into every single detail you've found out about each of them, tell me what your gut is saying?"

She inhaled a large breath and admitted, "I haven't quite narrowed it down to any one of them just yet."

"That's not helpful. You could have told me that over the phone, rather than meet up and hit me with it here."

"I'm sorry. I thought you'd want to hear where my investigation has led me so far."

Littlejohn groaned. "I can tell we're not going to get very far until you've revealed all." She glanced at her watch and said, "Get on with it. I can spare you twenty minutes."

Gee, thanks! Who's doing who a favour here? "Okay, I'll do my best to tell you everything in that time."

Littlejohn motioned with her hand to get on with it.

"Do you want to take some notes?"

The inspector pointed at her temple. "Whatever you say is retained up here, Miss Morgan. I have an excellent memory."

"I'm glad to hear it. My life can be full-on at times, hence the need to take notes."

"Yes, yes, we all know that you make a rod for your own back in your personal life. It shouldn't interfere with your professional life, though."

Ruth widened her eyes. *You're pushing your luck, lady.* Choosing to ignore the insult, she revealed the facts she'd discovered about each of the family members and the other people she'd interviewed.

Littlejohn refused to give anything away as she listened to what Ruth had to report. "I repeat, what's your gut telling you?"

"I know you're going to probably disagree with me, but my money is on a couple of the men I've come into contact with. The main one, I suppose, is Gerald Rattner."

"Isn't he the ex-policeman?"

"That's right. While I was questioning a member of the family, he was having a fight in the lounge with Zach Andrews."

"The ex-wife's new husband? Did you ask them what the fight was about?"

Ruth cringed. She'd been so intent on breaking the men up that she'd neglected to ask either of them that, or Cynthia and Reg after the men had been ordered out of the house. "I didn't. I can probably find out from Cynthia. It won't be until tomorrow, though. They're having a rest tonight."

"It's important. Why don't you ring them now?" Littlejohn smiled tautly.

Sighing and feeling as though she was backed into a corner, Ruth withdrew her mobile from her bag and looked up Cynthia's number.

Her friend answered within a few rings. "Sorry to disturb you, Cynthia, I'm with the inspector. I forgot to ask what the tussle was about between Zach and Gerald. Any idea?"

"Let me think. Nope, I can't seem to recall. I'll ask Reg, hold on a moment."

Ruth drummed her fingers on the table while she waited for Cynthia to get back to her.

"Ruth, are you there?" Cynthia asked.

"I'm here."

"Reg is under the impression that Gerald accused Zach of interfering, said he had no right to be there, and that's when things got out of control."

"Something and nothing really then. Okay, I'll let you get on with your evening. Thanks, Cynthia."

"You're welcome, anytime, you know that. I feel so much better now the house is empty."

"Glad to hear it. You shouldn't have to play hostess to those people, it's not as if they're your family. Speak soon."

Ruth ended the call and placed the mobile on the table beside her. "Minor detail from what I can see. Gerald accused Zach of interfering, and it all kicked off."

"Really? Seems strange. Okay, is that all you have? I know your suspicions are raised concerning Gerald Rattner. I'll get one of my team to dig into his background tomorrow. Has anything else shown up during your research today?"

"You might want to look up William Carter's past while you're at it. He told me he'd been in and out of trouble over the years. He didn't go into specific details, though."

"What about Belinda? Could this be an insurance claim murder case?"

"Again, that's probably something you should look into. I'm wavering about her. I've been told she has mood swings—that's true from what I've witnessed so far."

"Any idea why?"

Ruth shrugged. "Her age? I'm no expert on the menopause. She might be considered too old, that's the most likely scenario to me. Don't forget, she and Callum had an argument just before he went missing."

"There is that. What about Callum's ex-wife? Any feelings about her?"

"I didn't get anything. She and her husband, Zach, seem pleasant enough. They were there to support Julian, the son."

"And what about him?"

"He appears to be okay. As expected, he was upset about his father. At the end of the day, every single one of them did the right thing by dropping everything and showing up when the call went out."

"You're saying they should be admired for that?"

Ruth nodded. "In my experience, very few families ever do that. There are generally a lot of excuses flying around why people can't attend a family get-together when someone has passed. Don't forget, none of these people are local, as in, from Carmel Cove."

Littlejohn frowned and tapped a pointed finger against her cheek. "How far have they travelled to be here?"

"The farthest an hour, from Timbleton."

"Not too far. How many have taken the day off work?"

"Two, maybe three. Zach and Julian, not sure about William. I believe the others are retired."

Littlejohn sipped at her drink thoughtfully. "Nothing is really jumping out at me, if I'm honest. I'll make sure the team are aware of what you've divulged, and we'll do the necessary background checks. Anything else?"

"Not that I can think of, no."

The inspector finished her drink and stood. "Then I'll be off. Have a good evening, Miss Morgan. Again, I'm sorry things didn't work out for you and James. Maybe he'll get in less bother around the station now that he's not snooping for you." There was a glimmer of a smile in her eyes.

Ruth shrugged. "It is what it is. Life goes on as they say."

"That's the attitude. They're not worth it." She turned and walked out of the pub.

Ruth downed the rest of her drink and followed her out to the car park, her gaze drawn to the courtesy car she had at her disposal. Ben was staring back at her, his chin resting on the headrest of the driver's seat. She sniggered and looked up at the dark sky. She hated winter evenings, they made everything seem much more sinister in her mind.

Ruth dodged the small droplets of rain still falling and made it back to the car. "Come on, boy, a quick walk around the park and then home. I haven't got a clue what I'm going to have for dinner, though. Any suggestions?"

Ben whimpered and sat back in the seat.

"A great help you are."

After the brief jaunt around the park, sticking to the well-lit areas at all times, Ruth headed home. She dried Ben's feet with his doggie towel and prepared his dinner, consciously trying to ignore how quiet the house seemed to be. A single tear caught her out. She quickly swiped it away and got back to her chores.

Having decided on what she was going to have for dinner, she scrubbed a large potato, pricked it with a fork and popped it in the microwave, setting the timer for ten minutes—that should do. Then she opened a can of baked beans, poured half the contents in a saucepan and placed the other half in a Tupperware bowl in the fridge. While she was there, she removed the block of cheddar, grated a large handful and returned it to the fridge. She stood back, a smile covering her face at her swift achievement. *This cooking lark is simple, isn't it? All right, it might not be cordon bleu perfect, but it's good enough for me.*

Ben had cleared his dish and was already fast asleep in his bed in the corner. What more did she need? James' face drifted into her mind. Where had everything gone wrong? She could ask the same damn question over and over and still not know the real reason behind his rapid departure from her life.

She watched the timer countdown on the microwave and prepared her plate and cutlery for her culinary feast.

The house phone rang. She answered it after a few rings.

"Hi, babe, it's only me. What are you up to?" Steven's voice was a welcome distraction to her maudlin mood.

"Hey, you, I was going to ring you after I'd eaten. What are you up to?"

"I asked first."

"Just preparing dinner, nothing much. You?"

"At a loose end, hence the call. What's on the menu?"

"Jacket spud, cheese and beans. That's as exciting as it gets around here when I'm forced to conjure up something in the kitchen."

"Sounds fab. Will it stretch to two?"

"Sure. I can bung another tatty in the oven. How long are you going to be?"

"Thirty seconds. I'm parked outside."

"Nutter. You didn't have to ring. I'll open the door for you."

They remained on the phone, chatting until Steven entered the front door and removed his shoes.

Ruth busied herself in the kitchen, preparing another potato and adding the surplus beans to the saucepan before she grated another handful of cheddar. She made a note to go shopping in the next day or two to replace the staple ingredients she figured would see her through the next few weeks, until she got back on her feet and started flipping through her cookbooks for ideas, once the monotony of having jacket spuds with different fillings every night set in.

"Fancy one?" Steven dangled a bottle of red wine in front of her face.

"Will it go with our meal?" Ruth teased.

Steven roared. "No doubt it'll do wonders to enhance the flavour."

Ruth smiled. Her dear friend had managed to brighten her day already, and he'd only been in the house a few minutes. *If only he wasn't gay. What? Did I just think that?*

"That's like the old Ruth, always smiling. I hate to see you down. Why don't we eat dinner and you can tell me all your problems?"

She sipped at the wine he'd handed her. "I wouldn't want to bore you to tears. Anyway, I need cheering up, to avoid dwelling on matters which are out of my control."

He slammed his glass on the counter and grabbed her free hand. "Oh no, have you lost your ring? Where? When? I can help you hunt for it after dinner. I have a nose for detecting diamonds."

"No, I haven't lost it. It's sitting in the glove box in the car."

"For safekeeping?" Steven asked, confusion pulling at his brow.

"No. I was livid, tore it off and shoved it in there out of the way."

"Livid? Why? What's James done now?"

"He's only gone and told the folks at the station, his work colleagues, that we're no longer engaged."

His eyes bulged with shock. "Who told you that?"

"Littlejohn."

"Ha! And you believe what that witch tells you?"

"I have to believe it. Look around, Steven, do you see him here?" Tears misted her vision. "Damn, I don't want to cry."

He held out his arms, and she walked into them. "There, there, everything will turn out for the best, I'm sure it will. He'd be foolish to walk away from a beautiful person like you."

She took a few steps back and sniffled. "Thank you. I needed to hear that."

The microwave tinged. Ruth stabbed at the potatoes, checking to see if they were cooked—they were. Then she busied herself for the next five minutes, serving up the meal and avoiding any further conversation about James.

They ate in silence through the first half of their dinner.

"Is it all right?" she asked tentatively.

"Divine. What's not to love? I think the wine complements it beautifully. It captured the essence of the earthiness in the potato and the creaminess of the cheese superbly, don't you agree?"

She roared. "Having you in my life chases all the thunderous clouds away."

He glanced over his shoulder out of the back door. "Not sure how you can make that out—it's pitch-black out there. Hey, we'll go to our graves together as friends."

"Umm…I hate to tell you this, but I'm favouring cremation more and more these days."

"Whatever. Gosh, do we really have to talk about that over our sumptuous dinner?"

"Now I know you're winding me up." She raised her glass and clinked it against his. "To good friends, who are always there when you need a shoulder to cry on."

"Hear, hear. I'll drink to that. Right, what's for pudding?"

Ruth laughed and shook her head. "Same old, same old, always thinking of your stomach."

"Hey, if we didn't eat, we'd all be pushing up the daisies sooner than God intended."

"True enough. I think I have some ice cream stashed in the freezer."

"Anything but boring vanilla is fine by me. I'll start on the dishes." Steven cleared their plates and clattered them together in the sink.

Ruth cringed, fearing for the safety of her crockery.

Once the clearing up was completed, they moved into the lounge. Ben sat on the couch and snuggled into Ruth's hip.

"He's adorable." Steven ruffled Ben's head and he groaned.

"Maybe I should stick to having him as the only man in my life. It's definitely less hassle that way."

"That, in my honest opinion, would be a waste. James will come to his senses soon enough. He'll realise how much he loves you and crawl back home on his hands and knees, begging your forgiveness by the end of the week, guaranteed."

"I wish I shared your optimism. The question is: do I want him back?"

"Only you can answer that. Do you love him?"

"Honestly? Not when he behaves like this, walking out on me. What's that all about? I think anyone in my position would feel the same way as I do. All right, less about my boring lack of a love life, how are the preparations for the show coming along?"

"Slowly but surely. That's boring as well. What I really called round to find out about was your latest investigation. How's that going? Do you have an inkling who the killer is yet?"

She chuckled. "You're hopeless. I have a few suspects in mind." She spent the next ten minutes going over what had gone on the past few days. Steven listened intently without interrupting her, which was a first for him.

"Want to know what I think?"

"Go on then, free speech and all that."

"Charming. Okay, until you find this person who was seen running away from the beach on Saturday night, your investigation isn't going to go anywhere."

Ruth nodded slowly. "You're right. I'll jog Littlejohn's memory about that clue tomorrow. You're not just a pretty face after all."

"Get away with you. Here's another thing you might not have considered."

She shuffled in her seat, disturbing Ben in the process. "Sorry, Ben. Go on, you've got my attention."

"The son."

"What about him?"

"If he's super busy running his own business, it strikes me odd that he could spare the time to be here."

"Hmm...okay, I'll agree with you there to a certain extent; however, his father was the victim."

"Makes no odds, not to me. That's speaking from a man's point of view."

"You're insinuating all men think and act the same in these circumstances. Wait a minute, now you've got me thinking."

"And? What have you remembered?"

They clasped each other's hands as their excitement intensified. "He came on to me."

"What? Are you serious?"

"Yes, well, kind of. He said if ever I was in the area that I should drop by his microbrewery for a drink."

"And you saw that as him coming on to you?"

Ruth frowned. "Wouldn't you?"

He shrugged and expelled a large breath. "I'm not so sure. Maybe he was simply touting for business."

"It didn't come across like that to me, although, I suppose it did at the time. Meaning, I didn't think twice about it back then. See, that's the problem with this case, nothing is standing out as an obvious clue."

"Which is why it's imperative that you chase up what's happening with the guy on the beach. He's the key to all this, isn't he?"

"You're right. Without finding out who he is, everything else can be classed as insignificant. I'm glad none of them are staying at Cynthia's now. She and Reg need to grieve the loss of Callum in privacy. They couldn't do that playing host and hostess to the rest of the family."

"True enough. What's the wife like?"

She waved her hand from side to side. "I'm not sure what to make of her. It's her ex I have major doubts about."

"Why? Because of the way he treated you when he first showed up?"

"Isn't that enough? All I'm trying to do is ascertain the facts and find out who the killer is, and he made no attempt to disguise his hatred for me."

"For you? Or for your line of business? Take a step back and analyse things properly. Don't let a person's demeanour and their toleration, or lack of it, towards PIs cloud your judgement. While you're wasting energy disliking him and finding him suspicious, the real killer is laughing at you and lying low under the radar."

"You've got a point, or *two*. Maybe all this crap with James is affecting me more than I'm willing to admit."

"You're not wrong there. Consider what everyone has told you so far and go from there."

"Littlejohn asked me if I thought the wife had something to do with it, possibly so the insurance money came her way."

"And what do you think about that?"

"Not sure I agree with her. Saying that, Gerald was the one who showed up within hours of Belinda placing the calls. How many exes do you know who would drop everything to be by their ex's side?"

"True enough. Another angle you need to check on. Maybe they're in cahoots. He bumps Callum off and then moves back in with Belinda and they share the insurance money and live happily ever after."

A shudder suddenly ran the length of Ruth's spine. "Sounds callous and heartless to me. There again, it also sounds feasible. Grr…"

"Everything is feasible, surely, in a murder investigation. What about the ex-wife, what would she have to gain from Callum's death?"

"Nothing as far as I can tell. She's happily married to Zach. He seems legit, hence the reason I've crossed them both off my list."

"So, whittling it down, that leaves us with the brother and the son. You've already said you've got your doubts about the son. What's your instinct telling you about William?"

"I've asked Littlejohn to delve into his background for me. He told me himself that he's been in and out of trouble over the years, although he wasn't forthcoming with the details."

"Let's hope Littlejohn and her team find out soon. As an outsider looking in, I think it's strange that all of them should show up here. It reveals a couple of notable things to me."

"Which are?"

"Either the man was well liked or there's more at play here than meets the eye."

"You think there's some kind of conspiracy going on between a few of them?"

Steven shrugged. "Could be. On the other hand, I could be guilty of clutching at straws, which is why you're the PI and I'm the caretaker at the local school."

"Nonsense. Why do you always put yourself down like that? Your value in this community is so much more than that."

"Thanks. It still comes down to me slaving away at the school and running the am-dram club in my spare time to prevent me from going insane."

"You're amazing. If only the business was more stable, I'd give you a job without a second thought."

"Gee, thanks, Ruth, I'd love that. What a team we'd make."

"Look how you've forced me to analyse everyone and their motives when I was struggling to see the wood through the trees."

He stood and took a bow. "Okay, I'm going to call it a night now. I have a lot of setting up to do for the school governors' annual meeting tomorrow."

"Thanks for dropping by and supporting me."

"You're welcome. Now, do your best to track down the killer, and don't give James a second thought. He's the one in the wrong, not you. He'll come home soon enough."

"Whether I let him through the door or not, that's the dilemma I have if he does show his face anytime soon."

"You'll do what's right for you and Ben when the time comes."

They hugged at the front door, and Ruth stayed there to wave him off. Then she went back inside, let Ben out for his final toilet break and secured the house.

In bed, she read her Kindle, the new Tracie Delaney book called *Gridlock*, which she'd been looking forward to reading for a while. She fell asleep after only an hour or so, the Kindle clattering against her forehead waking her up. She then snuggled down under the quilt with Ben curled into her.

9

---

*T*he following morning, her head was dishing out its own form of punishment in the shape of a throbbing headache. She suspected the wine Steven had fetched was to blame. Ruth showered and dressed slowly, every movement an effort not to vibrate her head even more.

At fifteen minutes to nine, she headed into the office, stopping off at the park to give Ben his morning run. She was late this morning, and the dog walkers she usually spotted and chatted with were long gone by now. Even Cynthia was nowhere to be seen.

Once she'd arrived at the office and checked the post, which only included the obligatory invoice for her to pay someone in authority, she made her second coffee of the morning, knowing she'd probably feel much better after it had dripped into her system.

She was right. Feeling energised, she fired up her computer and trawled through the research she'd carried out the previous day on the family. Something was narking her, yet she couldn't place her finger on what that something was. By lunchtime, she was no further forward. Ruth glanced out of the window and, seeing that it was dry with dark clouds looming, she decided to take Ben for another walk. This time she drove up to the coastal path. The wind was lighter today, making the walk along the hilltop a more pleasurable one than they'd experienced in the past few weeks.

Her mobile rang as she and Ben were on their way back to the car.

It was Littlejohn. "I tried the office, you weren't there. Does that mean you're interviewing people or are you free to drop by the station for a quick chat?"

What if I bump into James? "I've just stretched my legs with Ben. I can be there in ten minutes. Is everything all right?"

"I'll reveal all soon." Littlejohn ended the call.

After she'd detected a note of excitement in Littlejohn's voice, Ruth raced the few feet to the car, started the engine and drove to the station in record time without going over the town's speed limit.

Leaving Ben in the back seat of the car, she took the lift up to Littlejohn's floor. The lift door opened, and she stepped out and immediately bumped into James.

"Sorry," she mumbled, her gaze latching on to his.

His expression proved difficult to read. "Hello, Ruth."

"James." She struggled to find anything else to say but his name.

"How have you been?" he asked, shuffling his feet on the grey office carpet.

"The same. You?" She tried to prevent the bitterness showing in her tone but failed. With her emotions churning, all she could think of doing was excusing herself from the fraught situation. "I have to run. I have an appointment with your boss."

"Heaven forbid that you should let me stand in the way of your work." He stood to one side and gestured for her to walk past him. "I'll see you around." He mumbled in her ear as she dashed past him.

Keep going, don't look back. I must keep moving. If I stop now, he'll know how much I miss him. I need to remain strong. This is down to him. He's the one who is going around telling everyone that the engagement is off, not me.

The lift door swooshed shut behind her. She thrust her shoulders back and marched towards Littlejohn's office, aware her presence was being scrutinised by the detectives sitting at their desks.

Littlejohn opened the door to welcome her. "Thanks for coming in so quickly. Can I get you a drink?"

Ruth waved the suggestion away. "I'm fine. I had some water in the car. What's up? I can sense you're excited about something."

"Several items. Take a seat."

Once they were both seated, Littlejohn tapped on her keyboard and swivelled her computer screen so that Ruth could see. "My team have been painstakingly trawling through the available CCTV footage we've managed to obtain from several of the shops in the area of the promenade. After viewing hours and hours of the footage, they discovered this snippet. It's not much, but I believe we could be looking at our killer here."

Ruth strained her eyes to distinguish the person in the dark. To make matters worse, they'd intentionally worn dark clothes. A black jacket with a hood. "Is that an emblem on the top?"

"If it is, it's too small to figure it out. Do you recognise anyone's physique? Could it be someone you've questioned in the past few days?"

Ruth exhaled and puffed out her cheeks. "I wouldn't like to say. It's not that clear. I'd hate to suggest someone, only for them to be falsely arrested." *Like Steven was* she was tempted to add.

"Okay. Let's leave that for now. My team have pulled out all the stops this morning and come up with some interesting facts. The main one concerning William Carter. His record is full of misdemeanours which have resulted in him serving time."

Ruth shuffled forward in her seat. "Go on. For what?"

"Theft, burglary. The incidents appear to be drug-related."

"Whoa! Are you telling me he has a drug habit?"

"That's what the evidence is suggesting. Could he have bumped his own brother off after Callum refused to give him money to fuel a drug habit?"

"Perhaps. Would it be worth having another word with him? Maybe if you spoke to him it would cause him to break down and confess."

"I was about to suggest the same. We've uncovered something else of interest, too. Something we've been waiting on for the past few days."

Intrigued, Ruth peered closer. "What's that?"

"The lady who spotted the person on the beach. We're presuming it's a man, nothing to suggest otherwise up to this point."

"Right, what have you got?"

Littlejohn messed around with her keyboard again and motioned to the screen.

Ruth gasped and shook her head. The likeness to one of the family members was unmistakable. "My God. Do you know who that is?"

"Yep. My own research has filled me in. I want to bring him in for questioning. Do you know if he's still here?"

Ruth shrugged. "I'm not sure. Do you want me to ring the hotel?"

"If you would."

Ruth had the answer they were looking for within seconds of ringing the hotel. "He's still there. No plans to leave as yet, according to the receptionist. I've asked her to call me if the situation changes."

"I'm thinking we should go over there and see what he has to say for himself."

"I'm up for that. The sooner we do it, the less chance there is of him absconding."

"Exactly. Do you want to come in my car or follow me over there?"

"I'll take my car, if that's okay. I have my dog with me. He goes nuts if I leave him. That sounded daft—I mean, if he saw me take off somewhere else and left him behind…oh gosh, now I'm waffling. You don't need to hear all the trivial details of running my life around my dog."

"From what I hear, your dog might be the cause of your personal problems."

"No. James told you that?" Incredulity was rife throughout her body. *How could he tell a stranger that?*

"He may have skirted around the issue. Are you not aware how jealous some men can get where pets are concerned?"

"Not in the slightest. James has always been happy with the amount of affection I've bestowed upon Ben in the past."

"Maybe there was only room for one man in your life once the ring was slipped on your finger. I noticed you're no longer wearing it."

"No. It's in the car. I'm too upset to wear it. You shocked me yesterday when you informed me that he'd announced the engagement was over."

"Why? No, don't tell me he hadn't told you?" She appeared genuinely taken aback by the revelation.

Ruth nodded. "It's done with now. He's made his decision. I've never been the type to plead with a bloke to stay with me. Once a relationship has run its course, there's only one thing left to do: get on with your life. I'll be wary of opening my heart up to anyone else in the future."

"Sorry to hear that. I expected better of him. If it's any consolation, he's been wandering around here like a lost sheep. If it continues, I might have to bring him in here and issue another warning. That won't do his career any favours to have another black mark on his record."

"Want me to have a word with him?"

"It's no longer your responsibility. The man needs to grow a backbone and get on with his life. Isn't he the one who walked out on you?"

Ruth nodded.

"And yet you're the one who is willing to bend over backwards for him. I can't fathom you out sometimes. Correct that, a lot of the time. If a guy did that to me, I'd cut off his…okay, I'll leave the rest to your imagination. Needless to say, I wouldn't be very happy."

In spite of herself, Ruth sniggered. "I'll leave it then. Do you want to head over to the hotel now?"

"Yep, that was the plan. I'll get Kenton to join us. It'll be good to have some muscle lying around in case things get rough."

"One look from you would strike fear in most people, I can vouch for that."

They both laughed.

"Enough of this, we should go."

. . .

uth followed Littlejohn's car through the high street to the Carmel Cove Hotel. She joined the two detectives at the entrance. Maria, the receptionist, welcomed them with one of her friendly smiles.

"Hello, Ruth, it's good to see you again. What can I do for you?"

"Hi, Maria. We were wondering if it would be possible to see the Carter family and their friends."

"I think they're all in their rooms. Want me to check?"

"Not just yet," Littlejohn interjected, raising her hand. "Would it be possible to speak to them all together? As in, do you have a room vacant that we can use?"

Maria pointed. "I'll check with my boss." She left the reception desk and returned a few seconds later and gave a thumbs-up motion. "Yes, my boss said you can use the room behind you. That's the same room you used before, Ruth."

She peered over her shoulder. "Perfect, thanks, Maria. Can you ring them all and ask them to meet up in this room? Try and be elusive, don't mention the police are here to see them, if that's okay?"

"Of course. Make yourselves comfortable. Want me to summon up some tea or coffee for you?"

Littlejohn checked with her partner and Ruth first and placed the order for three coffees.

Maria nodded. "I'll get them ordered for you, they shouldn't be long."

The three of them entered the room and between them set about pulling the tables and chairs into a half circle.

"We'll sit here. We'll have the perfect view of everyone from this position," Ruth suggested.

A waitress arrived with their drinks and left the tray on the top table in front of Littlejohn. Ruth reached over to collect a cup and saucer and sipped at her coffee.

"Okay, they should be here soon, providing they haven't got anything to hide," Littlejohn announced.

"They should be intrigued enough to join us. Maria didn't mention who we were," Ruth replied.

Moments later, Marlene and Zach entered the room.

"Hello there. Take a seat, will you? I'm DI Littlejohn, and this is my partner, DS Kenton. You're aware of who Ruth Morgan is, I take it?"

Zach and Marlene nodded, and both turned to give Ruth a smile etched with worry.

"Nice to see you both again. Please, don't be nervous, all we're trying to do is ascertain the truth about what happened to Callum."

"We understand," Marlene said.

Belinda and Gerald were the next to arrive. Gerald's eyes narrowed the second he saw Ruth sitting at the table. She nodded and motioned for them to take a seat.

"Who are you, and what's this all about?" Gerald demanded.

"I take it you're Gerald Rattner. I've heard a lot about you, Mr Rattner. All I ask is for your patience. I'm the SIO on the case, DI Littlejohn, and this is my partner, DS Kenton."

"Patience? We've been sitting around twiddling our thumbs for the past few days. I think our patience is wearing exceptionally thin by now."

Littlejohn tilted her head. "Meaning what, sir?"

"Merely stating a fact, Inspector. Make of it what you will."

"To me, you're coming across as being super defensive. I've noted down Miss Morgan's perceptions of the dealings you've had with her so far and I have to say, you haven't done yourself any favours, sir. Ex-police officer or not, this has, and continues to be, a very important investigation, and from what I've been led to believe, you've done your very best to be nothing but obstructive. May I ask why?"

"I dispute that. Had you bothered to come knocking at my door, I would have willingly answered any questions you may have had. I refuse to deal with a non-professional who passes herself off as a private investigator."

"Someone whom I've learned to trust over the years, sir. She has more courage than most men I know, and her attention to detail is second to none."

Ruth was gobsmacked by the praise Littlejohn had heaped on her shoulders. *Wow! Well, who'd have thunk it? Littlejohn sticking up for little ol' me and singing my praises to boot, too.*

"In that case, I apologise to you, Miss Morgan. I shouldn't have taken my lack of trust for PIs out on you."

"I accept your apology, Mr Rattner. I'm willing to draw a line under what has gone on in the past and wipe the slate clean."

"That's magnanimous of you."

Ruth stared at him, trying to work out if his words were of a genuine nature or if he was being sarcastic. He appeared to be suitably embarrassed by Littlejohn's put-down.

The final two people entered together. Ruth was tempted to nudge Littlejohn's knee under the table when she spotted something suspicious about one of the two men. William stopped at the door mid-step. Ruth feared he was going to take off as he glanced at the three of them awaiting their arrival. Julian, on the other hand, smiled and mock-saluted Ruth and her temporary work colleagues.

"Take a seat, gents. I'm the local inspector in charge of the case, and this is my partner."

William hesitated in the doorway for longer than expected. Julian pulled out the chair next to his mother's.

Littlejohn cleared her throat and began. "Miss Morgan has been very productive, working the case with me and my team. She and I met up last night and this morning to discuss some issues about the case that were bothering us. All in all, we're pretty sure that we've identified who the killer is and that person is sitting in this room."

"What? Don't be absurd," Rattner said, launching himself to his feet.

"Sit down, Mr Rattner. Please try and rein in the melodramatics, it doesn't wash with any of us."

He grumbled something incoherent and dropped back into his chair. "Pray, why don't you tell us who you believe the killer is then?"

"All in good time. You see, the killer was foolish to leave so many clues..." Littlejohn's voice trailed off, adding extra impact to her words.

She had everyone's attention. Ruth scanned the group, deliberately avoiding the killer's gaze which appeared to be trained on her. Out of her peripheral vision, she noticed Kenton swivel in his chair, no doubt anticipating taking off after the killer if he decided to run.

"What clues?" Zach broke the silence that had descended.

"That's for us to know. We'll announce our findings when the case gets to court. Far be it for me to lay too many cards on the table at once, Mr Andrews."

He nodded, accepting her reasoning.

Littlejohn had brought a manila folder with her. She flipped it open and took out the image of the killer the CCTV had picked up from one of the shops. She slid it across the table for Ruth to pass down the line. "Do any of you recognise the person in this shot? I know it's dark. Try your best for me."

Ruth watched each of them glance up at one particular person in the room.

The killer.

Belinda gasped. "You? Why? How could you kill your father like that?"

The colour drained from Julian's face.

His mother sobbed beside him and shook her head. "This can't be true...you didn't...why? Julian, say something...tell me they've got it wrong."

Julian shrugged and mumbled, "If that's what you want to hear, Mother. I did it. I'd been in contact with him for weeks. I asked him for money. He said he was going to cash in one of his investments for me, a bond that was due to mature. I arranged to meet him here on Saturday. Things went wrong between us." He glanced in Belinda's direction and sneered at her. "It's your fault he's dead, no one else's."

Belinda gasped and clasped the edge of her jacket at her breast. "My fault? How?"

"If you hadn't had a barney with him, he'd still be here today."

Ruth intervened. "How can you accuse Belinda when she wasn't even there, Julian?"

"He'd had enough. Her always arguing with him. Her mood swings are legendary, and he couldn't stand it any longer. It was one argument too many." He glared at her. "He told me he was leaving you. That he wanted a peaceful life in his retirement, not one filled with angst and destructive arguments."

"What did that have to do with what happened on Saturday night, Julian?" Ruth asked.

"He told me he'd cashed in his investment. He raised my hopes of getting myself out of debt only to snatch it away from me. The investment was a hundred grand. He said that after careful consideration he'd decided to keep the money himself and leave her. That cow, she's the one who killed him."

Belinda sobbed, and Gerald swooped in to comfort her. "Don't listen to him, Belinda. He's striking out because he got caught."

Julian tipped his head back and laughed. "Yeah, listen to that crazy ex of yours, like you always do. Have you any idea how much Dad hated him and the fact you run to him when you have a problem? Why else would he be here? Dad had a point, right?"

"Why are you doing this, Julian? Admit your guilt without causing any more unnecessary upset," his mother stated, seemingly horrified by his confession. "Why go to your father for money?"

Julian laughed again. "As opposed to coming to seek a handout from you and Zach here? Then what would you do for kicks, with no money left in the bank to prevent you from taking off on holidays at the drop of a hat? Isn't that the excuse you gave me when I reached out for help?"

His mother held her head in shame. "We've worked hard for that money. At our time of life, it's imperative for us to enjoy ourselves. Honestly, I didn't believe enough in your business to want to help you out. I bet, truth be told, we all felt the same way."

"And there we have it. What a supportive bunch you are. There I am, trying everything under the sun to sustain my business, knowing that it will grow exponentially within the next few years if trade is anything to go by, and you lot can't see further than your own front door. You lack the necessary skills to run a successful business…"

"So do you, apparently, if you needed a hundred grand," Ruth butted in.

"You know nothing, Miss Morgan. The money was to pay for new equipment I'd shelled out for, which in turn would triple the output. As it turned out, the money I had set aside wasn't enough to buy all the equipment. So, for your information, the business wasn't really in debt. The money was to ensure the business grew according to the demand. Dad was guilty of dangling the carrot. He assured me that money would be mine. I would have paid him back within a year, but he still refused to hand the money over."

"So you killed him," Littlejohn said.

His chin dipped to his chest. "I didn't mean to. It was his decision to test my nerve. He told me if I beat him to the top of the boulders then he'd consider handing over fifty grand. I figured half the money was better than none. Neither of us bargained for what would happen next. I didn't kill him as such. I was there when the accident occurred. The rain was battering the beach that night. Dad made it to the top of the rocks first—he knew he still had it in him to beat me. He took pleasure in that. When we both reached the top, he stumbled on a jagged part of the rock. It was dark by then, and neither of us could see what was going on at our feet. He toppled backwards. I tried to catch him; he was too far out of my grasp. I stayed with him, tried to stop the bleeding from the back of his head, but it was no use. He died in my arms."

"And you left him there? Didn't even bother to ring for an ambulance or the police? Why?" Littlejohn demanded.

"I knew I would get the blame for his death. You have to believe me, it was an accident. I could never have killed Dad. He meant too much to me."

"What about the money? You told us you were angry that he'd reconsidered your deal," Ruth asked.

"I was angry, it's true, but I could never have killed him. She's the one who did this." He pointed at Belinda.

"I...it was a simple argument, that's all. We would've got over it, we always did in the end."

Julian groaned. "Don't you get it? He was going to leave you."

She shook her head. "He never said a thing."

"Because you always stormed off. You never allowed him to have a voice of his own, ever. He was a shadow of his former self since he married you. He wasn't happy with you. By the time he realised how much Mum meant to him, she'd moved on and married Zach. There was no way back for him. He wasn't about to settle for second best, not that you come anywhere near that. Who wants to spend their life arguing over the merest of things? No one, that's who, and Dad definitely didn't. Yes, this is all down to you, woman."

"That's enough," Gerald shouted. He turned to Littlejohn and demanded, "Are you going to let him get away with speaking to Belinda like that? Arrest him and get him out of here. He's done enough damage as it is already."

"Thank you for the advice, Mr Rattner, I'll arrest him when I'm good and ready. Maybe you can explain why you're here?"

"Because Belinda called me, needed my help."

"Was there something going on between you and Mrs Carter?"

"No. How dare you suggest such a thing?"

His response was quick, almost too quick for Ruth's liking. "Belinda? Is that true?"

Belinda stared down at the tissue she was threading through her fingers. "No. We'd become close again recently."

"Belinda, don't say any more," Gerald warned.

Littlejohn tutted. "Looks like there's more than one of you to blame for the confusion running through Callum's mind before his death. Had he not been bombarded with all the problems hanging around his shoulders, maybe his attention would have been sharper and he wouldn't have fallen. I hope you're all happy with the outcome. We're going to need a full statement from you, Julian, stating the events of Saturday night. I won't be pressing charges, in light of what you told us."

Ruth faced Littlejohn and nodded her agreement.

Kenton left the room to summon uniformed officers to come and take down everyone's statement.

Littlejohn asked Ruth to join her in the corner of the room.

"Thanks for all your work on the case. I'm not sure any of this would have come out if you hadn't dug into everyone's background."

Ruth smiled. "I think you're being kind there. It was the CCTV footage that led us to this conclusion. I didn't get a bad feeling about him being a killer. Although I think he should be punished for leaving his father there, alone in the dark. There's every chance the man was still alive."

"I'll ring the Crown Prosecution Service and seek their advice on that one. Thanks again for your help, Ruth."

Her heart swelled. She was amazed that Littlejohn had thanked her for a job well done. That would have been unthinkable six months before.

EPILOGUE

*A*fter wishing everyone well, Ruth left Littlejohn and Kenton to do their jobs while she dropped by the Old Station House to break the news to Cynthia and Reg. They were both shocked and appalled by Julian's confession but also relieved that the truth had finally come out.

Ruth left her client's house and stopped off at the park to give Ben his usual run. Then she drove home, her thoughts still on the case and its surprising conclusion. She opened the front door and stopped. In the distance, she heard voices coming from the kitchen. Holding Ben's collar, she walked through the house to find Carolyn and James sitting at the kitchen table.

"Hello, what's going on here?"

Carolyn smiled. "Hi, I thought I'd drop by and see you and found this one sitting in his car outside. I hope you didn't mind us making a drink. I guessed you'd be home soon."

"I see. What do you want, James?"

Carolyn left her chair. "I'll be on my way. Let you two talk things over for a little while."

Her sister hugged her and nipped out of the back door.

An awkward silence settled in the room. Ruth busied herself by switching on the kettle to make a coffee. She turned around to see James making a fuss of Ben. "He's missed you."

"Has he?" James glanced up, and their gazes locked for the briefest of moments. "Have you?"

The kettle switched off. She finished making her drink and returned to the table without answering him.

"Have you?" he repeated, once she was seated.

"I might have done."

"Can we discuss what has gone wrong between us?"

"If that's what you want."

"I do." He reached over and tipped her chin up with his finger. "I've been an absolute idiot. I still love you, Ruth. I've been miserable the last few days. I need you in my life."

"Is that why you told Littlejohn you had called off the engagement?"

"I didn't. Not in so many words. She presumed that's what I was getting at." He raised her left hand. "You took your ring off."

"Only after having the chat with Littlejohn. I was angry that you should tell her without informing me. Is it worth continuing our relationship?"

He sank back in his chair as if an Exocet missile had struck his core. "Of course it is. I love you, Ruth."

"Do you? Do you *really*? Are you truly committed to this relationship? You've changed significantly since that ring went on my finger."

"I dispute that."

"You see, we can't even agree on that."

"All right, I admit that our lives haven't been going in the direction we'd hoped. That's because I'm desperate for you to become my wife."

"You have a funny way of showing it. You're the one who walked out, not me, James."

"I know. I regret my actions more than I can say. Won't you give me another chance, Ruth? Or have your feelings changed towards me?"

She spun her mug on the table a few times while she contemplated her answer. "I still love you, but what I won't accept is your childish behaviour." He went to speak, but she raised her hand to stop him. "There's no point in you denying it. To storm out of the house wasn't manly of you in the slightest. It was the action of a five-year-old. I won't tolerate such tantrums, James," she admonished him in her best headmistress's voice.

His head bowed, and he mumbled an apology, "I'm sorry, please, you're right and I was in the wrong. I love you more than life itself. It's taken me moving out to realise that, Ruth. Please find it in your heart to forgive me."

A lump developed in her throat. His pleading sounded pitiful but heartfelt all the same. He sat forward and gathered her hands in his.

"Please, you're the moon to my stars. The beach to my sea. The grass to my garden."

"Oh, please, please stop. I can't take any more." She smiled and nodded. "One last chance. We give it six months. If things remain the same, as in, strained between us, then I think we should call it a day and move on. Deal?"

"Deal. You won't regret it. I'll change, for the better, I promise." His sincerity won her over.

They shared a loving kiss which sealed the pact. "I will say one thing, James. Don't ever speak to me like that again, not if you want to hang on to the dangly bits between your legs. I refuse to be treated like some downtrodden wife or partner, you hear me?"

"I swear, I'll never be that nasty again."

"Now, what's for dinner? I've missed your culinary skills if nothing else." She sniggered.

"You cheeky mare. I knew you'd miss something about me not being around."

"Make me a feast worth savouring, and you'll get into my good books quicker."

He pecked her on the lips again and rushed over to the freezer. "Will steak and chips with all the trimmings do for now, until I can stock up the fridge?"

"Sounds fabulous to me."

"Congratulations on solving the case, by the way."

"Thanks. In the end, Littlejohn and I were able to put our differences to one side and solve it between us."

"You're the talk of the station. It made me proud to hear Littlejohn speak positively about you for a change. It made me realise you're not a bad sort after all."

She reached for the tea towel on the back of a nearby chair and aimed it at his head. "Glad you saw the light, eventually."

THE END

NOTE TO READER

Dear Reader,

What a heart-wrenching read that was.

But as usual, Ruth came to the rescue one of her dearest friends and even managed to work alongside DI Littlejohn, wonders will never cease.

Look out for more from Ruth Morgan in 2020

In the meantime, perhaps you'll consider reading one of my thriller series? Have you tried the DI Kayli Bright series yet?

Here's the link to the first in the series **The Missing Children**

Thank you for your support as always.

M A Comley

Reviews are a fantastic way of reaching out and showing an author how much you appreciate their work – so leave one today, if you will.

Printed in Great Britain
by Amazon